"Perhaps the pretty widow feels like being...merry?"

He brushed the knuckles of one hand against her cheek in a caress that was contemptuous rather than provocative. "Perhaps it gets lonely around here in the long winter evenings."

"Yes, I am a widow, and yes, the house does seem lonely—very lonely—without my husband. But I'm not looking for someone to replace him...not even for one night. And if I were, I doubt very much if you would even make it to the shortlist. There would be little comfort in going to bed with a man who is as totally devoid of human warmth as you appear to be."

GRACE GREEN was born in Scotland and is a former teacher. In 1967 she and her marine-engineer husband, John, emigrated to Canada, where they raised their four children. Empty-nesters now, they are happily settled in West Vancouver in a house overlooking the ocean. Grace enjoys walking the seawall, gardening, getting together with other writers...and watching her characters come to life, because she knows that once they do, they will take over and write her stories for her.

Don't miss any of our special offers. Write to us at the following address for information on our newest releases.

Harlequin Reader Service
U.S.: 3010 Walden Ave., P.O. Box 1325, Buffalo, NY 14269
Canadian: P.O. Box 609, Fort Erie, Ont. L2A 5X3

GRACE GREEN

Snowdrops For A Bride

Harlequin Books

TORONTO • NEW YORK • LONDON
AMSTERDAM • PARIS • SYDNEY • HAMBURG
STOCKHOLM • ATHENS • TOKYO • MILAN
MADRID • WARSAW • BUDAPEST • AUCKLAND

For Jennifer

ISBN 0-373-11694-2

SNOWDROPS FOR A BRIDE

Printed in U.S.A.

CHAPTER ONE

A BONE-CHILLING February wind screamed down from the north, whistling over the cemetery adjacent to Glencraig Parish Kirk. It flung hissing sleet against the headstones and caused the two giant pine trees at the entrance gate to wave their branches in frantic protest.

Strome Galbraith stood alone, his tall figure rigid, in front of a small granite cross. He barely noticed that his black hair was being tossed about by the gale as he directed his gaze over the words chiseled on the speckled stone:

Hazel Dunbar, dearly beloved wife of Hugh Dunbar...

She had died a year ago, he saw. A year ago, almost to the day. And she had been only thirty-three.

He rammed his hands into the pockets of his black cashmere coat, and his lips twisted cynically.

She had been only eighteen when she'd had her pre-wedding fling with him. Only eighteen when she'd given him three weeks of her life—twenty-one days . . . and one perfect night.

Only twenty-one days, only one night, but they had changed his whole life. *She* had changed his whole life, had changed *him*...from a man who had given his heart passionately and without reservation, to the man he was now, a man with no heart to give.

And when he had recently learned the extent of her betrayal, and the callousness of it, his old anger had flared anew from the long-dead ashes, bringing with it memories he'd believed he'd extinguished years ago, memories that still, incredibly, had the power to wound.

"Bitch!" he muttered under his breath. And, "Bitch!" again, louder this time. Exhaling a sigh that seemed to be dredged up from the very depths of his soul, he brushed a trembling hand across his eyes. Why in heaven's name had he come to the cemetery? Certainly not to pay his respects, for respect was not a word he associated with Hazel Dunbar. So what had drawn him so inexorably to——?

"Are you all right?"

He froze at the sound of the soft, concerned voice with its lilting Highland cadence. His imagination must be playing tricks on him! For a mad, senseless moment he'd thought it was a voice from the grave...

He swiveled around abruptly, shock still rippling through him. It was almost with relief that he saw not a ghost, but a flesh and blood figure standing right behind him—a tall, slender young woman in a beige trench coat and high-heeled brown boots. Her hair was concealed by a kerchief knotted at the throat, its jade silk framing an oval face with delicate features and ivory skin that was almost translucent. There was a weariness in her wide-spaced, violet blue eyes, but there was also a glimmer of warmth as they fixed on him anxiously.

"Are you all right?" she said again, hunching a little against the wind. "I was wondering if——"

"Of course I'm all right." Because of his bitter mood, and because she'd caught him by surprise, there was a harshness in his voice that wasn't really directed at her, and he felt sorry about that. "Why shouldn't I be?" He tried to sound less hostile.

The thickly lashed blue eyes regarded him steadily. "I saw you looking at Hazel's grave." A drop of sleet trickled down her small, straight nose. "Did you know her?"

Know her? No, he thought self-derisively, he didn't know her. Hadn't ever known her. He shrugged and avoided answering the frank question. "I'm just interested in old graveyards." Quickly, before she could pry any further, he changed the subject. "I'm planning to stop over in the area for a few days—can you recommend a decent hotel?"

A tiny frown puckered her brow, and he saw her take quick inventory of his expensive coat, his fashionably narrow dark pants, his handmade Italian leather shoes, before she said, "You won't find one in Glencraig, but there's an excellent little inn about forty miles farther up the glen. You can't miss it—it's called the Heatherview. Right on the edge of the moor."

"Thanks," he said. But as he turned to go he noticed, with a faint stirring of curiosity, that she was cradling something in one arm, to protect it from the wind. Her glance followed his, and he saw her lips curve in a small smile.

"Snowdrops," she explained. "I'm taking them to my husband's grave—they were Rory's favorite flower." Her eyes lifted to his. "He and Hazel were killed in the same accident—a runaway truck slammed into a crowd of people on the High Street. The two of them died instantaneously. Six others were hurt...among them Hazel's husband Hugh. He had head injuries and was in a coma for several months before he died. He did come to, just before the end, and we all hoped for Kilty's sake that he was going to make it, but——"

"Kilty?"

"Hazel's and Hugh's son. They only had the one child. He's fourteen, going on fifteen—and he's finding life very difficult, I'm afraid. It was so hard for him, losing his parents, and then having to——"

She broke off with a grimace. "I'm sorry—you can't possibly be interested if you didn't know Hazel! And I've been prattling on and keeping you standing here in the cold. It's not a day to be out of doors! I hope you find the hotel to your liking..."

As she turned to leave the wind snatched at her kerchief, pulling it off her brow a little, and he caught a fleeting glimpse of shining auburn curls before she tugged the silk square back into place. The movement released the faintest hint of some fruity perfume, its fragrance scenting the air for just a second before the wind stole it away. And then, with a friendly smile and the casual lift of one hand, the woman passed by him, walking away along the narrow path with an energetic but graceful stride. In a moment or two she turned a corner, and disappeared from view behind a high, neatly trimmed hedge of holly.

Strome Galbraith turned up the collar of his coat and, heedless of the sleet needling his face, stared again at the modest granite cross, unseeingly this time, the stranger already forgotten, but her words echoing in his head...

Kilty. So they... someone... had given the boy a nickname. Had probably given it him as a child, and it had stuck—as nicknames tended to do, he knew, in this part of the world. His face softened in the beginnings of a smile, but before it reached his eyes he compressed his thin lips tightly. He had come here to *see* the boy, that was all. To verify that he was, indeed, his son. And, if he was convinced of that, when he got back to London he'd contact his lawyer, and have his will changed, making the boy... this Kilty... his heir. That would be the right thing for him to do.

But that was the only thing he was going to do.

He certainly didn't intend getting involved, certainly didn't intend revealing to the boy that he was his father. There was no room in his life for family, for people, for emotion. For heartache.

Only fools laid out their hearts to be trampled, he reflected bitterly as he turned his back on the grave of the woman he'd once loved.

And he was no longer a fool.

"I've brought you snowdrops, Rory."

Crouching down, Nairne scooped out a handful of moss on the sheltered side of her husband's gravestone and nestled the delicate white flowers in the earthy hollow. "The first of the year." She cupped the moss around the fragile stalks, making them safe from the wind's grasping claws, and as she did she felt her throat muscles constrict. She and Rory had had a February wedding, and in each of the seven years of their marriage he had brought her from their garden at Bruach the first snowdrops of spring, and the lovely, shyly drooping flowers had come to symbolize the purity, the steadfastness, the simplicity of their love. Now she felt her heart ache painfully. Who could have guessed that one day she would be bringing them to him...and so soon?

"The boys have all gone to the Outward Bound school, darling." Her words were a mere whisper, snatched away by the wind almost before they were uttered. "And this year I arranged for Kilty to get time off school so that he could go too. The bus came for them this morning while it was still dark. Bruach's going to be so quiet for the next three weeks... No one left but Shadow and me."

She swallowed the lump in her throat as she hugged her arms around herself tightly, rocking a little. "Oh, Rory, the last year has been so hard without you..."

I will not cry. I will be brave. I will go on.

She slowly straightened, and brushed away the threatening tears with the back of her hand. "I have some decisions to make," she said in a husky voice, "and I intend making them while the boys are away. But I don't want to talk about that today. When I've thought it all through I'll come back and tell you everything.

"I must go now. Kyla and Adam are coming over for dinner, and I've a lot to do before then. See you next time."

Tenderly, as if the smoothly hewn gravestone were a living thing, she ran the chilled fingertips of one hand across its surface, and then stood for several long mo-

ments, her eyes closed. Finally she turned away, and
began to walk back along the path.

As she rounded the edge of the holly hedge she noticed
the sound of a car engine starting up outside the cemetery gates, and, over the wail of the wind, seconds later
heard the crunch of wheels spinning on the gravel as the
vehicle took off. The dark stranger, she reflected . . .

How out of place he'd seemed, in his sophisticated
city clothes. She'd expected to have the cemetery to
herself, and it had given her quite a start to see him there,
so dark and brooding . . . like a character out of some
Gothic novel. Odd that he'd halted his journey on such
a stormy day, just to poke around an old cemetery.

And he'd looked so lost, so . . . alone. She'd wanted to
reach out and smooth the bitter lines twisting his lean
features, wanted to ask him who had hurt him in the
past, who had caused him to look at the world with eyes
so bleak and empty——

Oh, Nairne, she chastised herself with a sigh of mock
despair, don't you have enough problems of your own
right now, without wanting to solve everyone else's?

Bowing her head against the slanting sleet, she called
to the black collie waiting patiently under one of the
pine trees, "Good boy, Shadow—let's go now," and,
lengthening her stride to keep up with her eager companion, she set out for home.

"Your roast was done to perfection—as always, Nairne."
Kyla Garvie rinsed the last crystal wineglass, and, drying
it carefully, put it in the cupboard with the others before
turning to her sister, who was placing a small tray on
the countertop. "Now," she took Nairne by the shoulders
and pointed her in the direction of the door, "go and
keep Adam company—the two of you haven't had a
chance to chat for ages. I'll see to the coffee. Should I
put out some cookies?"

"I baked some shortbread yesterday—you'll find it in the——"

"Shortbread? Oh, won't Catriona be delighted? She loves your shortbread. I'll put a couple on her special plate... She should be here in a little while——"

"She's coming over? Kyla, why didn't you tell me? I assumed the children were at home and Molly baby-sitting!"

"But I did tell you!" Kyla stared at her sister. "Didn't you get my message on your telephone answering machine? I phoned this afternoon, but you were out——"

"I went to the cemetery."

"Yes, that's what I thought when you didn't answer, but I left a message—said Mom and Dad would be driving Kevin and Catriona to the church hall for the Sunday School party, and their teacher would drop them off here afterward."

"I didn't get any message." Nairne frowned. "How strange, Kyla. Of course, I checked my machine after I got back from the cemetery, but I'd forgotten to turn it on before going out, so there was nothing——"

"No, dear, you didn't forget to turn it on—I left a message for you——"

"But there *was* no message. Honestly——"

"Perhaps you erased it by mistake."

Nairne shook her head. "No, I didn't."

"Perhaps it was the goblins, then!"

Nairne chuckled, remembering how, when she was a child, she'd scraped a palette knife over an oil painting their mother, Kate, was working on, and when asked who might have done it she'd whispered that it must have been the goblins.

"You couldn't have forgotten to turn it on." Kyla's words were firm. "I *definitely* left a message."

"Then why didn't I get——?" Nairne's words were interrupted by the sound of the doorbell ringing, and she stared at her sister. "Who on earth can that be?"

Kyla glanced at her watch. "Probably Kevin and Catriona... though I didn't expect them quite so soon." She made for the door. "I'll be right back."

As she heard her sister's high heels trip across the hall Nairne crossed the kitchen to the windowed alcove where she kept her desk and phone. She had switched on the answering machine when she'd come home from the cemetery, and the red light now shone steadily, depicting that there had been no messages left since then. With a click she switched it off and set the tape to rewind, and immediately it clicked into place. There was nothing on the tape... but what on earth could have happened to Kyla's message...?

Anyway, no harm was done. Adam and Kyla were here and the children would be coming into the kitchen any minute now—four-year-old Catriona running excitedly, her dark curls bobbing; Kevin, twelve, the serious one, following with a quiet smile on his face.

Nairne hummed under her breath as she placed mugs on the tray. Family. How fortunate she was to be part of a warm and loving family—her mother and father, Kyla and Adam, Kevin and Catriona... What she would have done without them after Rory's death she didn't know... and of course having the boys working around the place, in and out all the time, had helped too——

"It wasn't the kids after all!" Kyla breezed back into the kitchen, her long black hair swinging around her shoulders as she moved. "It was just someone looking for a place to stay. He saw your B and B sign—I guess the gale flipped it over this afternoon, so it was showing the 'Vacancy' side, instead of 'Closed for the Season.' Thank goodness the wind's died down now—it's not too bad a night." Her scarlet blouse shimmered under the fluorescent light as she reached up into the cupboard and took down the tartan tin where Nairne kept her shortbread. "I said he'd find nothing in Glencraig, told him to go on up the glen to the Heatherview, but he said he'd already tried there—had dinner there, actually—

but there was a big wedding on today and every room was taken——''

Nairne paused, one hand curved around the sugar bowl. "Oh, dear..." She bit her lip. "Not a tall, dark man—rather nice-looking, with a clipped English accent——?''

"Mmm. He did have a wonderful BBC accent—and such a sexy voice!" Kyla stared at her sister. "But how on earth did you know?''

Nairne closed her eyes for a moment, ignoring Kyla's astonished question. The man wouldn't find a place to stay between here and Inverness, not at this time of year; he'd be on the road for hours, and a bleak and lonely road it would be...

" 'Rather nice-looking' " must be the understatement of the year," Kyla was saying. "The man is gorgeous!" and added with a sigh of pretended despair, "Sometimes I think that when I was born I got all the passion that was allotted to our family, so that when you came along there was none left, and God gave you an extra share of beauty and sweetness and serenity to make up for——''

Nairne hadn't been listening to the words flowing around her. She made a sudden decision. "Here, Kyla, take this!" Thrusting the sugar bowl at her startled sister, she spun around and sped from the room. It was probably too late to catch him, she knew, but the grounds were large and the driveway circular, and if she took the short cut through the stand of pine trees that stood between Bruach and the front gate she might, she just might, get to the road before him.

Without bothering to grab a jacket from the hall cupboard, she snatched open the front door and, slamming it behind her, leaped down the flight of shallow sandstone steps. Kyla was right, she noted in a distant part of her mind as she sped across the graveled area in front of the house and darted along the darkly shadowed path among the trees, it wasn't a half-bad night now.

The wind had died down, and, though wet drops spattered over her as she brushed against the lower branches of the trees, the sky was clear, and there was even a bit of a moon.

By the time she emerged onto the drive again her breath was rasping in her throat, and she could feel her heartbeats hammering wildly. But when she saw the low outline of a powerful car halted at the gates, its motor idling, she put on an extra spurt. She reached the vehicle just as it was starting to pull away. Running around to the driver's side, she hammered on the window with her fists. When the car jerked to a halt, she pulled back, hugging her arms around herself.

The window slid down automatically, and the driver leaned sideways against the door, angling his head up so that he could see her. In the shadowy darkness she could make out little more than the glitter of his eyes.

"What the devil——?"

"Sorry if I gave you a fright." Shivering as the cold, damp air seeped through her blouse and made the silk fabric cling to her skin, Nairne stooped so that her face was almost level with his. "You came to the door just now looking for a place to spend the night, and Kyla—my sister—turned you away. As she told you, I'm not open for business—but you're welcome to come back if you want. You'll not find anywhere else for miles."

In the pause that followed her words Nairne became aware that his car radio was playing. Not music, but some program about finance; she heard the announcer say, "... and the stocks we recommend in the short term are——"

He snapped off the radio. "I wouldn't want to put you out."

"You won't," she assured him. "And I feel rather guilty for having sent you all the way to the Heatherview this afternoon and wasting your time—I forgot about the Kilmartin wedding——"

"Ah. The woman at the cemetery..."

"Mm. I run Bruach as a B and B in the summer, but it's no problem for me to get a room ready for you tonight. It's not as fancy as the Heatherview, of course, but..."

She heard a click, and before she could wonder what it was he said, "Hop in, and I'll drive you up to the house."

She realized that the click was the passenger door being unlocked. "Oh, there's no need."

His voice held a hint of impatience as he said, "If you walk then I'll just have to wait for you when I get there, won't I?"

Obviously a type-A personality, Nairne thought wryly. "All right," she returned. "Thanks."

The car—a top-of-the-line Mercedes—must be a recent purchase, she decided as she got in and sank back in the passenger seat. It had the unmistakable, pleasant smell of new leather. Added to it, she noticed, was another very faint, very elusive scent—the male scent of the man driving it. Not the outdoor, earthy smell she had come to associate with Rory, but a very sophisticated, spicy fragrance, probably originating in a bottle of super-expensive cologne purchased at some elegant city store— maybe even Harrods! But certainly not at their popular annual sale. This wasn't the kind of man who would line up to save a few pounds, that much she felt sure of, even from the little she'd seen of him.

"Do you have any luggage?" she asked as he drew to a halt between Adam's Rover and her own white van.

"Just one bag. It's in the trunk." He flicked on the roof light, and reached between the two seats to get his coat from the back seat. As he twisted around again his shoulder brushed against Nairne's, and for a fleeting moment she felt the warmth of his body through the silk fabric of her blouse. She pulled back quickly, as if she'd been stung, her eyes sweeping involuntarily to his.

Her throat muscles inexplicably tightened. Kyla was wrong, she thought, "gorgeous" doesn't even begin to describe this man. Fascinating, intriguing, ruthless—the words drifted like a fog into her mind, clouding it as, in one breathless glance, she took in the lean, hard-angled face, the piercingly intense blue eyes below the dark slash of eyebrows, the beautifully sculpted lips that somehow managed to combine strength, inflexibility and sensuality. His hair was as black as the blackest night, with not the slightest sprinkling of gray, though the lines etched around his eyes and the creases bracketing the chiseled mouth set his age, she guessed, at around forty.

Why had she not noticed these things when they'd met at the cemetery? Had she been too taken up with the bleak emptiness in his eyes...? Eyes that were now looking into her own in a way that sent a disturbing sensation tingling right through her——

"Sorry," she heard him mutter, and with a quick, jerky gesture he rubbed his shoulder. Trying to ignore the sudden racing of her pulse, Nairne followed the movement. But, even as part of her mind was registering the soft luxury of his charcoal gray cashmere sweater, another part was still stumbling, bewildered by her reaction to him, a reaction set off by the accidental brushing of his arm against her own.

Abruptly she opened her door and got out. As she waited at the top of the steps while he took his suitcase from the trunk she forced herself to analyze her response, and analyze it honestly. And as she faced the truth she felt guilt hit her like a sharp slap in the face. She'd reacted the way she had because his touch had disturbed something in her that had been sleeping for the past twelve months. What she'd felt had been nothing more, nothing less than a stirring of desire.

Oh, how shameful, that she, who was scarcely yet used to her widowhood, could be turned on, and so quickly, by a complete stranger.

She shivered, biting her lip as the tall figure mounted the steps and joined her. Turning away from him, she opened the door and led him into the hall. As she closed

it again Kyla and Adam came out of the living room
together, their expressions questioning.

"Oh," Kyla chuckled, "you went after him! I told
Adam I thought that was where you must have gone."

Without letting her eyes meet those of the stranger,
Nairne took his coat from him, and turned away to hang
it in the cupboard. She took advantage of the breathing
space to regain control of herself, and when she turned
it was with clear eyes and a casual smile. "Yes," she
said lightly, "that's where I went...and I caught him
at the gate as he was waiting to make a right turn onto
the road." She noticed that the stranger had dropped
his bag just inside the door, and she went on, "Let's go
through to the fire. I'm freezing—you were right, Kyla,
it's quite a nice night, but still very cold."

As they all walked into the large living room Adam
said, "Nairne, have you and your new houseguest in-
troduced yourselves yet?"

"No, though this is the second time we've met. We
bumped into each other at the cemetery this afternoon."
She directed a level glance at the tall stranger, and held
out her hand. "I'm Nairne Campbell."

After only the briefest hesitation he murmured,
"Strome Galbraith," and clasped her chilled fingers in
his warm grasp. As flesh met flesh, again, to Nairne's
dismay, she felt the same distinct shiver of sexual excitement she had felt when he'd brushed against her in
the car. But this time she was a little better prepared for
it, and managed to keep her voice steady as she drew
her hand from his strong, firm fingers and in turn in-
troduced Kyla and Adam.

Her gaze flickered over him as his attention was diverted to the others. She had to admit that she had never
seen the like of him in Glencraig before—and not only
because of his exorbitantly expensive clothing. Power
and command were in every line of his bearing, from
the rigid set of his wide shoulders to the harsh strength
of his rugged features. Lean, tall, muscular, he was the

kind of man who would test every boundary to the limit, the kind of man who wouldn't suffer fools gladly...

The kind of man who would be hard to get to know.

Now where had that last thought come from? she wondered. And yet she was sure she was right. His body language spoke clearly of an invisible wall he'd erected around himself—you can come so far, it said, but I will permit you to come no farther. He was probably quite unaware, Nairne decided, that when she'd looked into his eyes at the cemetery she had for a moment seen through a chink in that wall, to a bleak and lonely place where she knew no one would be welcome——

"...so I'll go and get the coffee, Nairne."

As her sister's words broke into her thoughts Nairne forced her lips to curve into a smile.

"Thanks, Kyla." Making a casual gesture towards the hearth, with its cheerily glowing fire, she said to the other two, "Shall we sit down?"

"If you'll excuse me a moment," Adam said, "I'll take a turn down the drive and see if the children are coming."

He followed Kyla from the room, and as the door shut behind them Nairne found herself toying nervously with her gold wedding ring, aware of the silence in the room now that she and Strome Galbraith were alone. Strange...she'd always thought the living room at Bruach was huge; tonight it seemed to have shrunk, its dimensions diminished somehow by the mere fact of this man's presence. And it was a long time, she reflected uneasily, since she'd felt such an unfamiliar awkwardness in a situation like this.

Taking a deep breath, she gestured toward a large, comfortable armchair. "Do sit down."

He remained standing where he was, a few feet away from her. "I'd prefer to go straight up to my room. It's quite obvious I'm intruding on a family get-together." He rubbed a hand over his nape, the gesture conveying a weariness that his crisp tone had not.

"Oh, please don't worry about that! You're not——"

The door opened before she could continue, and Kyla came in, bearing the tray with the coffee things. "Here we are. Adam's taken Strome's suitcase upstairs, Nairne—I told him to put it in the wee bedroom above the kitchen and put a match to the fire." She placed the tray on the coffee table. "It is the warmest room upstairs, isn't it, at this time of year?"

"Yes, it is," Nairne said with a rueful smile. "The bed's right above the Aga cooker! Thanks, Kyla. Now, Mr. Galbraith, you will have a coffee with us, won't you, before you go up?"

"Oh, you can't go upstairs yet—you must try Nairne's shortbread!" Kyla kicked off her shoes and curled up in a corner of the sofa. "She's won first prize three years running at the Glencraig Farmers' Show—— Ah," she tilted her head as the sound of laughter came from the front hall, "there are the kids!"

No sooner had she spoken than the door burst open, revealing Adam, Kevin and Catriona. The dark-haired little girl pushed her way past her father and her brother, her cheeks flushed with excitement. Hurling herself across the room, she stopped in front of her mother, small hands starfished on Kyla's knees. "Daddy says Auntie Nairne made shortbread." Her gray eyes sparkled. "Can I have a piece?"

"Where are your manners?" Kevin, who had come up behind her, tugged one of her black curls and smiled teasingly. "And where will you find room for shortbread after eating all those Smarties the minister gave you?"

Catriona whirled around, her lower lip jutting out in a pout. "You ate most of them, you know you did!"

"But you'd already picked out all the red ones—and you knew those were the ones I wanted!"

Adam and Kyla laughed, but Nairne's smile died away as she happened to glance at Strome Galbraith, the uneasiness she'd felt earlier coming back in a rush when she saw the expression on his face. He was standing back a little from the happy family scene, and his mouth was set in a grim, hard line. She hadn't noticed before, but his skin seemed to be too tightly draw over his cheekbones, giving him a haggard appearance. What a contrast it made, she realized with a heavy, sinking sensation—on the one hand the close-knit members of her family, laughing, animated, at one with the cheerful atmosphere in the room—a room which itself had a pleasant ambience, with its rose carpet, white walls and chintz-covered furniture—and on the other this grim, remote stranger. Even his clothes—his charcoal gray sweater, dark pants and black shoes—were a somber contrast to everything around him.

Just as Nairne moved forward to ask him again to join them he turned, and she found her eyes locked with blue eyes so bleak that she had to use every ounce of her self-control not to whisper aloud "Oh, dear Lord..."

And as he opened his mouth to speak she knew—instinctively—what he was going to say.

"No," she shook her head, her throat so tight that her voice was scarcely a whisper, "no, you mustn't go. It's far too late to be on the road looking for a place to stay."

She was aware that the others were still bantering and laughing over by the hearth, was aware that for the moment they'd forgotten about the stranger...and, moved by an impulse that she couldn't resist, she closed the space between the two of them, and put a hand on his arm.

"Come with me," she urged. "I'll show you your room."

She thought he was going to reject her offer. She saw the hesitation flicker across his face as he looked down at her slender hand, the pale, slightly freckled skin, the oval nails innocent of polish. Feeling her cheeks turn warm, she dropped her hand.

After a long moment he nodded, tersely. "All right. Thank you."

Unnoticed, they went out into the hall, and Nairne closed the door behind them, before crossing with him to the stairs. There wasn't room for two abreast, so she walked slightly ahead of him, holding the banister rail lightly as she went.

Before she was halfway upstairs she felt as if every nerve ending in her body was tingling. He probably wasn't even looking at her, she told herself tautly, but she was intensely aware of his presence behind her. She felt her cheeks become even warmer as she imagined his dark gaze trespassing over the feminine curves of her waist and hips, over her trim buttocks as they moved under the seat of her gold skirt, over the toned muscles of her calves and the slender grace of her ankles, set off by her sheer nylons.

As she reached the landing she tried to pull herself together. Her imagination was working overtime, that was all it was. This man was far too wrapped up in his own unhappy little world to be the slightest bit aware of her as a woman. There wasn't even a full moon, for heaven's sake, and yet she seemed to be going a little bit crazy!

Forcing her lips into a casual smile, she turned to usher him to the left toward his bedroom...

But he had assumed they would be going to the right.

Her smile froze in place as she collided with a wide, muscled chest, her breasts crushed against him, her nostrils subjected to the intimate male scent from his darkly tanned skin, his thick black hair, his warm breath...

He automatically grasped her by the upper arms to steady her...but, though he steadied her body, his move did nothing to steady her heartbeats. Instead, they thundered wildly in a way that was totally new to her...and in a way that brought to her mind a fleeting image of the historical romance, *Desire's Dark Dawn*, that was sitting on her bedside table. Was this the electrical physical attraction that Esmeralda, the young heroine, felt when Bragan, the pirate hero, touched her that first time...this dizzying, mind-dazzling, floating sensation? It was something she'd never experienced before...

With a protesting gasp she pulled herself free.

"I'm sorry." Oh, Lord, where had that husky, breathy voice come from—surely not from her? But it must have done, for it had brought a quick frown to the stranger's brow, and a surprised light to his blue eyes...blue eyes that, even as Nairne watched, became cynical.

"A room for the night," he said in a tone that was light but held an unmistakable note of warning, "is all I want, Mrs. Campbell. Nothing more."

Nairne stared up at him, hardly believing her ears. Had he thought she had bumped into him on purpose? Was *that* what he was implying?

Despite her flaming auburn hair, she was normally slow to anger, but now she felt a swift burst of temper flare inside her—temper mingled with incredulity. This stranger was obviously misinterpreting her reasons for offering him shelter. Well, she had better set him straight!

"And a room for the night," her expression as she looked up at him was a carefully calculated mixture of astonishment, wide-eyed innocence and gentle reproach, "is all, Mr. Galbraith, that I'm offering!"

Sidestepping him, she walked with long, graceful strides along the hall to the little bedroom above the kitchen. Flinging open the door, she stood aside, and with a curt gesture ushered him inside, hoping he wouldn't notice the hot color in her cheeks.

"There you are," she said, fighting a sudden and totally uncharacteristic urge to hit him as he walked by her. "It's small, but it's warm and comfortable. Breakfast will be at eight, if that's all right with you?"

"Eight will be fine." He looked around the cozy room for a moment, before walking across the cream carpet to the fireplace, where he stood with his hands in his pockets, his eyes fixed on the sputtering fire in the antique-tiled grate. There was all of a sudden such an aura of loneliness, of unhappiness around him that Nairne's anger gave way to a sudden surge of compassion.

She hesitated a moment, feeling a little stab of remorse for her artificial behavior of a moment ago...and feeling a strong urge to say something that would open the path to honest communication between them.

But she could see by his expression—which was once more dark and brooding—that he had already forgotten she existed. His mind was on problems that were of far more importance than the reality around him.

With a small sigh of regret Nairne stepped out into the hall, and closed the door soundlessly behind her.

CHAPTER TWO

BRUACH was almost three hundred years old, and built of sandstone. The roof was slate, the wooden window frames white-painted, and the walls two feet thick. Before moving into the house, Rory and Nairne had had central heating installed downstairs, but had decided they couldn't afford to do the same upstairs. So, except in summertime, the bedrooms were always cold; they had fireplaces, but those were lit only in the case of illness, when an invalid had to be kept warm.

Or, as was the case tonight, if there was a guest in the house. Mr. Strome Galbraith, Nairne mused wryly, would no doubt be as cozy as pie in his bed above the Aga cooker and with his coal fire crackling in the grate!

With a shiver she snuggled under her duvet, trying in vain to get warm. When Rory had been alive she'd never felt cold in bed, but this winter it was different. She'd been promising herself for weeks now that she'd get herself an electric blanket, but she'd kept putting it off, knowing that there were other things she needed more.

Tonight she was sure there was nothing on this earth she needed more! Brief as her run through the trees had been earlier on, she had become thoroughly chilled, and, though she'd huddled in front of the living room fire for a half hour or so after Kyla and family had left, she still felt chilled to the bone. She drew her knees up and, dragging the hem of her nightie around her numbed feet, peeked at the digital alarm clock that sat beside the framed photo of Rory on the bedside table...

Almost midnight——

What was *that*?

24

Nairne held her breath. Such a crash, such a thud! As if someone had knocked over a lamp and then fallen headlong to the floor on top of it!

Without stopping to think, she clicked on the bedside light and, shoving aside the duvet, jumped out of bed. There was no one in the house except for herself and Strome Galbraith. What on earth could have happened? Had he fallen? Had he hurt himself? Or, heaven forbid, had he had a heart attack?

Before getting into bed she'd spread her Viyella robe over the duvet for extra warmth; now she snatched up the green tartan garment, and speared her arms into the sleeves as she ran across the room. She'd left a dim light shining in the upstairs lobby when she'd turned in, and now in its shadowy rays she hurried toward Strome's room.

She'd intended knocking sharply on his door and calling his name, but when she reached the door she hesitated. What if the noise hadn't come from here? What if he was asleep? He wouldn't thank her for rousing him in the middle of the night.

She decided, instead, to ease the door open and peep in. No need to switch on the light—the glow from the fire would surely let her see if he was all right or not.

She curled the fingers of her right hand around the polished wooden doorknob and turned it slowly, carefully.

The hinges creaked just a little, and she grimaced. Sssh, she whispered to herself, and tried not to think of how cold her bare feet were. Drawing in a deep, shivering breath, she began to push the door inward.

She'd barely moved it two inches when it was opened from the inside with a jerk. She gasped, but before she had time to step back Strome Galbraith appeared in the doorway, his dark figure looming over her.

He hadn't stopped to put on a light, but he hadn't needed to, because—as she had guessed it would be— the room was lit by the flickering flames in the fire. She could see that his black hair was disheveled, and the navy robe belted around his lean, muscular body had obviously been hastily thrown on.

"What the *devil* do you want?" he demanded, his hands on his hips.

The relief Nairne had felt on seeing him upright rather than horizontal on the floor dissipated swiftly when she heard his hostile, accusing tone. She peeked past him and saw that the brass lamp still sat securely on the bedside table, and a further, lightning-swift glance around the room showed her that nothing had been disturbed. His suitcase stood by the wardrobe, a sleek leather wallet lay on the dresser by the door, but, save for those and the tangled disarray of his bedcoverings, there was no sign that the room was even occupied. Mr. Strome Galbraith, Nairne reflected, was a tidy man.

He was also, at this moment, a very angry one.

"I thought I heard a noise," Nairne said quickly. "No...I *did* hear a noise. I heard a crash, like something breaking, and then a heavy thud, like a body falling on to the floor. I thought something had happened to you——"

"How strange." She noticed that his expression had subtly changed. The irritation compressing his lips had gone, to be replaced by a smile...a smile that didn't reach his eyes. "I myself didn't hear a thing!"

"But you must have," she protested, "unless you were asleep."

"Mrs. Campbell, I'm a very light sleeper. I can assure you that if there had been any sort of a crashing sound it would have wakened me."

"Then..." Nairne's words trailed away as the fire in the small room erupted in a series of sharp hissing explosions. Of course, that could explain why he hadn't heard anything. "The sound of the fire crackling must have drowned out the noise——"

"Or," he leaned indolently against the doorjamb, "perhaps there *was* no noise. Perhaps..."

A second before he went on she knew exactly what he was going to say. Knew exactly why he thought she'd come knocking on his door at midnight.

"Perhaps it gets lonely around here in the long winter evenings," he said softly. "Perhaps you just wanted a little...company." Before she could anticipate what he was planning to do he brushed the knuckles of one hand against her cheek in a caress that was contemptuous rather than provocative. "Perhaps the pretty widow feels like being...merry?"

Nairne stepped back, feeling her skin burn where he had touched it. "Mr. Galbraith," she somehow managed to keep her voice steady, "I don't admire a man who expresses himself in euphemisms. I believe in blunt talk. If you think I came to your room because I wanted to have sex with you, then why don't you just come right out and say so?" Suddenly realizing that she had clenched her hands into fists and her nails were digging holes in her palms, she flexed her fingers and thrust her hands roughly into the pockets of her robe. "I'd much prefer that to your insulting insinuations. But I'll respond to them anyway. Yes, I am a widow, and yes, the house does seem lonely—very lonely—without my husband. But I'm not looking for someone to replace him...not even for one night. And if I were I doubt very much if you would even make it to the short list. There would be little comfort indeed in going to bed with a man who is as totally devoid of human warmth as you appear to be." There, she had said what was on her mind; if she had gone too far it couldn't be helped.

Her feet felt like blocks of ice; it was only with a great effort she got them to move. Turning from him, she began to walk back to her room. She held her breath as she walked, half expecting that at any moment he would call to her and apologize. But he didn't.

A few moments later she was back in her bed. And now she knew for sure that she wouldn't sleep. Oh, not only because she was even colder than she had been before her disastrous little excursion, but also because of the inexplicably unsettling effect her houseguest had on her.

A room for the night, he'd said. Well, that meant only one night. And it was just as well he'd be leaving after breakfast—it was as plain as the nose on her face that the man had problems. Major problems. And she already had more problems than enough to cope with—trying to manage Bruach without Rory's help and worrying about finding enough work to keep her troubled teen-agers busy in the off-season—without taking on someone else's. Given enough time, of course, she was sure she could help the stranger—or at least get him on the road to helping himself. Something from his past, more than likely, was eating away at him, and till he brought it out into the open and faced it squarely he'd never be able to get on with his future.

With a sigh, Nairne squirrelled right under the duvet, and, rubbing one cold foot briskly against the other, over and over again, forced the man right out of her mind and concentrated on imagining that she was somewhere hot—a tropical beach, on a sultry afternoon, with the sun blazing down on her heated, oil-slicked skin...

It seemed like forever before she began to warm up, though warm up she eventually did. But just as she was finally dropping off to sleep a disturbing thought popped into her head and brought her wide-awake again with a jerk. Wide-awake...and more than a little alarmed. If Strome Galbraith wasn't responsible for that crash in the night—and she had no reason to believe he was lying—then who was?

Had the noise come from the attic? Perhaps the gale had blown a window in and knocked something over! That would certainly account for the crash she'd heard, followed by the heavy thud. She should really go and look...

With a moan Nairne squeezed her eyes shut and pulled the duvet right over her head. Dark attics weren't her thing. She certainly wasn't about to look for a flashlight and climb that narrow, winding staircase alone, certainly wasn't about to poke around among all the creepy shadows up there, not knowing what she might find! And there was no way she was going to ask Mr. Strome Galbraith to accompany her, not after the reception he'd given her just a short while ago.

She'd wait and check the attic out in the morning. *After* he had departed.

The kitchen was warm, the air redolent with the smell of crisply grilled bacon and freshly brewed coffee, when a low growl deep in Shadow's throat warned Nairne that her overnight guest was on his way downstairs.

Forcing a smile, she turned from the Aga, heated plate in one hand, spatula in the other, to find that he was already standing in the doorway, looking startlingly masculine in a black turtleneck sweater and black, tightly fitting pants, with his dark hair brushed carelessly back. Her heart did a little quickstep as she saw the look in his striking blue eyes; by turning around so abruptly she had caught him unawares, and for just a second she thought she had seen a flicker of sexual awareness in his quickly hooded gaze.

She must have imagined it, she told herself self-deprecatingly as she uttered a brisk, "Good morning." What could he possibly see in her that would attract him? She was certainly not the kind of elegant city woman he would be accustomed to—just a country lass with overly long legs, an overly generous bosom, and an over-abundance of curly red hair that was the bane of her life! Then what was it about his presence that made her so uneasy? Why was she all at once so intensely aware of her appearance, so aware of the skintight jeans she always wore to work in, so aware of the emerald green sweater that for some reason seemed to be pulling against her breasts every time she breathed? Relax, she ordered herself, he's going to be gone soon enough. She'd feed him and send him on his way, and once she'd changed his bed and cleaned his room it would be as if he'd never existed. She could just forget all about him.

"I usually feed my B and Bs in the dining room," she said, "but, since you're by yourself, I thought you wouldn't mind eating here in the kitchen. It's so much cozier in winter." With the spatula she gestured toward the round, bleached oak table. "Help yourself to coffee," she went on, "and I'll be right with you."

In an effort to sound casual she hummed lightly under her breath as she arranged six rashers of bacon alongside two perfectly fried eggs, mushrooms, and grilled tomatoes. The best thing to do, she decided firmly, was to pretend that last night had never happened.

She turned, expecting to find him sitting at the table, but he had taken up his stance at one side of it, his back to her, and was looking out of the window.

Nairne cleared her throat, and, walking across to lay down his plate, said, "A change in the weather this morning. It's like spring. I wore my heavy jacket when I was out earlier, and by the time I came home I had taken it off—I was quite warm enough in my sweater."

He turned, and she saw that his skin was even more deeply tanned than she'd realized. The dark color seemed to intensify the piercing blue of his eyes. "You've been out already?"

"Mm. I take Shadow for a wee walk every morning."

"A 'wee' walk?" His thin lips twisted. "And how far would a 'wee' walk be, Mrs. Campbell?"

Nairne glanced down at Shadow, whose tail had been thumping on the floor since his name was mentioned. "We walk to the other end of Glencraig, and along the loch aways—it takes about...oh, an hour. It's probably four miles or so in all."

"Ah," his tone was mocking, "so that's a 'wee' walk." He half turned and, looking outside again, gestured toward the nurseries stretching out to his right. "You have a market garden?"

"Mm." Thank goodness he seemed prepared to act in a civilized manner this morning, and had obviously decided, like herself, to put last night's unpleasantness behind him. She pulled out a chair for him, and then rounded the table. It amused her to see the flicker of surprise cross his lean features as she sat down; had he expected that she, like a servant, would wait, and eat when he had finished? Catching her lower lip in her teeth to hide her smile, she poured two mugs of coffee, and, waiting till he'd sat down, leaned over and placed his by his setting.

"Now," she said as she took a triangle of toast and spread it generously with lime marmalade, "you were asking about the gardens. I should explain the whole setup here. It's a two-part operation, really—the house being one part, the gardens the other. My part is the house—in the summer, as I've told you, I run Bruach as a bed and breakfast. Rory and the boys always looked after the gardens, growing fruit and vegetables for sale mainly down south, but——"

"The boys?" Strome frowned, and paused with a forkful of tomato halfway to his mouth.

"My husband and I were both involved in social work for the district before I inherited Bruach. We set it up as a private concern, and have always employed juveniles—first-time offenders—who have been recommended to us through the courts. We give them a job, and training, the understanding being that once they're ready they'll leave and get a job in the open marketplace, leaving a slot here for someone who needs it more than they do."

"How many boys do you have just now?"

Nairne sipped from her cup before answering. "Seven at present—eight if you count Kilty," she added absently, "though his situation is different. But they're not here at the moment."

For some reason that Nairne couldn't fathom, the tension in the room suddenly seemed to tighten. She put

her cup down and unobtrusively searched the face of the
man sitting across from her. He had just put a piece of
bacon in his mouth, and seemed to be taking forever to
chew it. When finally he'd swallowed it he laid his fork
and knife on his plate and sat back.

"The boys aren't here?" There was a studied casu-
alness in his tone that was completely belied by the
tautness of his features. "Where are they?"

"They're somewhere on the west coast—I don't know
exactly where, as they're on a sailing ship. It's an
Outward Bound venture—they'll be away for three
weeks. The project is sponsored by the district, and you'd
be amazed by the change in every one of these lads after
three weeks on the open sea. They come home with such
a pride in themselves, in their accomplishment, and for
some of them it's a first..."

Her voice trailed away. She'd lost him; she could see
by the distant look in his eyes that he was no longer
listening to her. For a moment she felt a flare of irritation—directed not only at him, but also at all the other
people in the world who were bored by teenagers and
their problems. Could they not see that by ignoring these
problems, by not treating them at their roots, society
was going to be faced by even more serious problems in
the years to come?

Abruptly Nairne pushed back her chair, and with a
weary sigh swept back the mass of auburn curls tangling
over one shoulder. Unless a miracle happened, even the
small part she was playing in trying to solve these
problems was going to come to an end, and very soon,
now that Rory was no longer here to share the load with
her. She and the boys had somehow managed to carry
on without him last summer, but now spring was almost
here, and she knew she couldn't put off making her decision much longer. It was just not going to be econ-
omically feasible to carry on at Bruach without him. And
hiring someone had proved impossible. Oh, she'd inter-
viewed a couple of social workers, but had found no one

who also had gardening skills, marketing skills, mechanical skills, and all the other skills Rory had possessed, skills that had kept their expenses to a minimum. She sighed, and got up from the table.

"Excuse me, won't you? Do help yourself to more coffee and toast if you want..."

"No, I've got to get going. An excellent meal," he added—tersely, as if he knew the right words to say but didn't have access to the right tone in which to deliver them. He shoved his chair back and got to his feet. "If you'll just give me my bill..."

Nairne had already prepared the bill, and she lifted it from the countertop and handed it to him. Expectantly she watched him slide a hand into his hip pocket, then watched a frown flicker across his face. "I've left my wallet upstairs."

"Why don't you go up and collect your things? You'll find me in the kitchen when you come down."

Nairne cleared the table, and, filling the sink with warm water, squirted some liquid soap into it. Not worth using the dishwasher for just two people, she decided, and, slipping on a pair of rubber gloves, quickly began washing the plates and cups. She was just placing a cup on the plastic dish rack, when she heard Strome's step in the hall. It sounded, somehow, angry. Shadow growled and, getting up from his warm spot by the Aga, loped across to Nairne. Frowning, she took off her gloves and bent to pat his head. "Ssh," she whispered, "it's all right——"

"It's gone!" Strome Galbraith's eyes were spitting fire. "My wallet was sitting on the dresser when I came downstairs, and now...it's gone!"

"But it can't be—you and I are the only ones here! It must have slipped down the back of the dresser or——"

"Don't you think I've already checked?" His response was almost a snarl.

Nairne tried to keep cool; this man had an abrasive manner that rubbed her up entirely the wrong way...and entirely too easily. "Let me just go up and double-check," she said in as steady a voice as she could manage.

As she hurried along the lobby she could hear his steps right behind her, could almost feel the heat of his angry breath. Good grief, where could his wallet be? she wondered anxiously.

And why the devil had she run after his car last night? Why couldn't she have let well enough alone! Kyla had *told* him she only took B and Bs in the summer...so what had made her take off after him the way she had? This man was causing her more problems than all her other B and Bs put together!

His bedroom door was open, and Nairne strode right in. Her glance immediately zoomed to the top of the dresser where she'd seen the wallet the night before and——

"Good Lord!" she snapped. "Your wallet's right there, in front of your eyes! How could you have missed it?" Swiveling around, she stared up at him accusingly. "What exactly are you playing at?"

She had to admit, he looked taken aback. No, that was putting it mildly; he looked absolutely stunned. If it was an act, she decided, it was a damned good one.

"But..." He shook his head, raked a hand through his black hair. "I could have sworn..."

"Right, Mr. Galbraith," Nairne said crisply. She picked up the wallet and tossed it to him. "You don't look like the kind of man who tries to get away without paying his bill, but that kind of man never does, does he? Would you mind checking that nothing's missing?" Tilting her chin, she glared at him.

Tension twanged between them as he riffled through the notes in the wallet, and through his collection of credit cards.

"Nothing's missing," he said flatly.

What did you expect? Nairne wanted to retort. Instead, she just said, "Good," and, holding out her hand, added coldly, "Now if you'll just pay me, and take your coat and bag and leave, we'll forget the whole thing ever happened."

He seemed to be in a daze. Without uttering one more word, he took the notes from his wallet and paid her, and crossed to pick up his suitcase. He opened his mouth as if to say something, but when he saw the look of censure in Nairne's eyes he obviously decided that there was no point.

Within a few minutes she was ushering him out of the front door, and with a very curt, "Goodbye," she closed it firmly behind him. There, she thought, that's the last I'll see of Mr. Strome Galbraith.

And thank goodness for that.

He was the kind of man, she thought as she leaned back against the door with her eyes closed and listened to his car disappear down the drive, who would cause disruptions wherever he went. There was a restlessness about him, and it would provoke a restlessness in others.

At least, it had provoked it in her, she admitted. And she didn't like it. All she wanted, now that Rory was gone, was peace, and the chance to be alone with her memories.

With purposeful steps she went upstairs, and set about ripping the sheets off Strome Galbraith's bed. And, after throwing them in the washing machine, she went back upstairs and cleaned out the fire in his room. Once she had it set again to her satisfaction, and had washed all the soot and ashes from her hands, she knew she could put off no longer the task she had been dreading all morning.

CHAPTER THREE

THE attic at Bruach ran the full length of the house and access to it was by a flight of narrow wooden stairs spiraling up from an alcove on the second floor.

As Nairne climbed up the gloomy steps she whistled loudly. She wasn't nervous as a rule, but she found herself wondering if it mightn't be a good idea to start keeping her front and back doors locked... yet it went against the grain. Bruach had always been open house to the teenagers working there, a refuge they could seek, day or night, when they couldn't handle things at home; it wasn't unusual for Nairne to come downstairs in the early morning and find a dead-to-the-world figure curled up with Shadow on the rug by the Aga. But Rory was no longer with her, she was a woman living on her own now, and it might be wise to be more cautious in future.

Meanwhile, she reminded herself with a grimace, there had been that dreadful noise last night, and the boys were many miles away, and couldn't have been responsible for it. But she knew she wouldn't rest till she'd found out its origin... which would be, she told herself sternly, something as simple as a mouse having knocked over an old lamp.

Wrapping her arms around herself, she began prowling around, but it took her only a few minutes to fully convince herself that no one was hiding among—or in!—the boxes and old trunks crammed under the eaves. Only one place left to look—she felt her pulse quicken—the small room in the tower at the far end, which held nothing but an antique brass bed that had apparently been used in days gone by when a live-in servant slept there.

Tentatively Nairne pushed open the door with her fingertips. The sound of its creaking hinges was loud in the silence, but as she scoured the room with a swift glance she exhaled a heartfelt breath of relief. No one there; of course, she'd known the room would be empty, but——

Oh, Lord! Nairne gasped, grasping her throat with her left hand. The room was undoubtedly empty...now. But someone had been here. And recently. She stared disbelievingly at the mattress, which had fallen through on to the floor—apparently the cause of the crash she'd heard—her eyes, wide and round, taking in the heavy gray army blanket lying in a rumpled heap in the middle. She almost didn't notice the empty cigarette packet tossed on the floor by the head of the bed, and the stubs and ash contained in a tin lid beside it.

Someone had been up here last night. While she had slept. Someone who had casually lit up—she counted— no less than five cigarettes, and smoked them. In her home.

Anger surged up inside her. Anger so strong that it swamped any feelings of fear. But somehow she knew that whoever had been here was no longer in the house. She sensed it, and her instincts didn't usually let her down.

Taking deep breaths, she drew back out of the room and closed the door. Take it easy, she told herself. There must be a simple explanation. And now at least she knew why Strome hadn't heard the noise—his room was at the very other end of——

The squeal of tires on gravel, followed immediately by the ear-piercing shriek of car brakes that had been applied with sudden, savage force, crashed into her thoughts, startling her. It sounded as if someone had hurled a vehicle to a halt, right at her own front door...and whoever was in charge of the vehicle, she decided, was obviously in one almighty rush. Was there an emergency of some sort?

Heart leaping, she scuttled across the attic. As fast as she could, she scrambled down the spiral staircase and sped along the landing. Down the main stairs she hastened, and just as she reached the bottom step the bell pealed. The sound was so unexpected that she gave a little shriek. "I'm coming!" she yelped, and, stumbling across the front hall to the door, she tugged it open.

"What...?"

She couldn't get anything else out—couldn't, had she been paid a fortune. The tableau that met her eyes was one she could never have imagined in a thousand years. Strome Galbraith was standing in front of her, his expression as explosive as if he'd just swallowed a charge of dynamite...

And by the scruff of the neck he was holding a youth—almost as tall as himself—whose face was pale, and sullen, and unwashed. A youth whom she recognized only too well, a youth she'd have recognized anywhere, for who else possessed that tall, lanky frame and spiked, purple-gelled hair? Who else wore a safety pin fastened through his left earlobe... and who else could combine with such grace an ancient Rolling Stones T-shirt and a ragged old Black Watch kilt that hung low on his lean hips and swung jauntily around his strong, muscular legs? Kilty Dunbar! Oh, dear Lord, Nairne asked herself in dismay, what was he doing here? Hadn't she just seen him off on the bus herself yesterday morning? He was supposed to be on the high seas in the Outward Bound sailing ship, the *Queen's Bounty*...

And what on earth could he have done to deserve the fate that Strome Galbraith obviously intended delivering to him?

Nairne swung the door wide-open and gestured with one outstretched hand. "Come in." Her voice revealed her utter bewilderment. "I think explanations are in order."

"Get inside!" With a rough twist of his arm Strome pushed the youth ahead of him into the hall, and Nairne saw his lips compress grimly as Kilty wrenched himself free and stumbled back against the carved oak hallstand.

"Explanations?" Strome's voice was hot with anger. "Ask *him* for an explanation. What's your name, boy? And don't play any more games with me unless you want me to call the police."

The boy's gray eyes were determinedly blank as he avoided looking at his questioner. He mumbled something that was unintelligible.

"Speak up!" Strome demanded sharply.

"Dunbar," the boy snapped with a fierce thrust of his jaw. His eyes were no longer averted from Strome; they were fixed on him defiantly. "Somerled Dunbar. My friends call me Kilty, but you," he added in an insolent tone, "are welcome to call me Somerled."

Nairne stared at the two, wondering which seemed more of a stranger to her. Kilty she'd known since he was born—his mother had been one of her dearest friends. Her heart had overflowed with grief for him when he'd lost both his father and his mother. But she'd never known the boy to be so rude. Strome Galbraith she'd known for barely twenty-four hours, yet, as she looked at him now, at the ghastly pallor of his face, in the midst of this bewildering confrontation between the two, somehow it was to him that her sympathy flowed. He looked as if he was ill, really ill...

"Would someone tell me what's going on?" she demanded. "Kilty, what on earth are you doing here? Why aren't you with the others?"

There was no insolence in his voice as he answered her. "I told Mr. Webster I wasn't feeling well. I asked if I could come back. He phoned to tell you——"

"I didn't get a call," Nairne broke in. "And there was none on my answering machine."

She saw his face color. "I erased it from your machine."

"What?" Nairne struggled to make sense of it all. "When?"

"I saw you leave for the cemetery yesterday, and I went in then. I didna want anyone to know I'd come back."

For a long moment Nairne could do nothing but stare at him. Then, as she began to put the pieces together, she said slowly, "So...it was you upstairs—in the attic—last night!"

Kilty dropped his gaze to the floor. "Aye."

Nairne shook her head. What on earth was going on? She turned her attention to Strome Galbraith, but when she saw his expression the question on her lips died away. He was looking at Kilty in a way that absolutely jolted her...and she realized that it was because he wasn't just *looking* at him, he was...staring at him with eyes that were a little wild, scrutinizing him—scrutinizing his face, scrutinizing it with a concentrated intensity that made the hair at her nape prickle. It was as if he was looking for something—something beyond Kilty's actual features. But whatever it was he was looking for, it was plain by the anger in his gaze that, if he was finding it, it was something he didn't want to see. Oh, she was surely being fanciful—or was she going out of her mind? Taking a deep, steadying breath, she said firmly, "Mr. Galbraith, I'd be obliged if you'd tell me how you're involved in all this."

At first she thought he hadn't heard her, and she was just about to repeat her question when—with an obvious effort—he dragged his gaze from the boy to her. For a moment there was a bewildered look on his face, as if he had forgotten for a moment where he was. Then gradually, as she watched, his expression cleared, his eyes became ice hard, and he seemed once again to be in control of himself.

He rammed his hands into his pants pockets and said curtly, "After I left here I found myself thinking about the noise you heard last night, and my wallet disappearing this morning. I put two and two together, and came up with the possibility that there might be someone else in the house. I thought I'd better let you know——"

"So you decided to come back."

"Right. And I was just coming through the gates of Bruach when I saw——"

"He saw me sneak out the front door." Kilty scowled at Nairne, and shuffled his feet in their large black leather Reeboks. "Sorry, Nairne."

"But I still don't understand." Nairne wove a hand wearily through her hair and pushed it back off her brow. "You were the one who took the wallet, Kilty?"

"I took it, but only to——" He broke off, and his lips clamped stubbornly together. He was obviously not going to explain *why* he had taken it.

"But you put it back, and apparently there was nothing missing. No money, or credit cards...?"

His eyebrows twitched nervously, and he shook his head. A jerky shrug of his shoulders was his only other answer.

An impasse. Nairne knew one when she saw one. With a sigh she turned to Strome. "*Are* you going to phone the police?"

"I don't see what it would accomplish," he said curtly. "But it's quite obvious to me that you're in no way capable of supervising this boy—goodness knows how you think you can manage eight of them...and run a market garden...not to mention a bed and breakfast in the summer. If you want my advice," he finished sardonically, "you'll sell this huge place and find yourself a nice young man and get married again. Settle down and raise a family—hopefully little girls who won't cause you too many problems."

All the sympathy Nairne had felt for him a moment before dissipated as if it had never been. Words of fury and resentment crowded to her lips, but somehow—she didn't know how—she managed to bite them back. Better not to speak at all, she decided irately, than give this

man the satisfaction of knowing how he'd upset her.
Staring steadily at him, she waited for him to leave.

But he didn't make a move. Instead, she saw a very
faint dark red color seep into his face, heard him clear
his throat, once, and again, and then, to her absolute
amazement, he said with just a touch of embarrassment
in his voice, "I was wondering, Mrs. Campbell, if I could
presume on your hospitality for a few more days."

Yes, Nairne thought, she was definitely going crazy.
Was this how Alice had felt when she'd found herself in
Wonderland? Curiouser and curiouser...

She tried to tell herself that if he hadn't taken her aback
by his sudden about-face, and if she hadn't been so
worried about Kilty and anxious to get him on his own
so that she could have a talk with him, she would have
smiled coolly and said in her most businesslike voice that
in the circumstances it would be better if he left. But she
didn't. Oh, she did smile coolly, but somehow, as she
looked up into black-fringed eyes that had become almost
navy blue in their intensity, she found herself hypnotized, spellbound.

"No problem." Had she really said that? A little voice
inside her head warned her that she was making a huge
mistake. She ignored it. Why, she had absolutely no idea.
Swallowing, she shifted her gaze from Strome to the open
doorway behind him. "If you'd like to get your things
from the car and take them upstairs, I'll put on a pot
of coffee. Give me... ten minutes."

Was it her imagination, or had he drawn in a deep,
relieved breath? Why had it been so important for him,
all of a sudden, to stay? Nairne forced her mind away
from him; whatever his problem was, it was *his* problem,
not hers.

In the meantime she had other things to do... and the
first was to have a talk—a private talk—with Kilty.

She turned away from Strome and, putting her hand
on the boy's arm, said, "Come on through to the
kitchen, Kilty."

Ten minutes. She hadn't given herself much time...but surely in that time she could talk with him, find out what was wrong. She didn't believe that he had come back because he hadn't been feeling well; what she did believe was that for some reason he hadn't wanted to go away on the ship. He had wanted to come home.

But why?

Would he tell her?

"Have you eaten today?" Nairne poured cold water into the coffeemaker, tilting her head around as she waited for Kilty's answer.

"No, I havena."

"Are you hungry?"

"Aye."

"Then I suggest that, as soon as you've told me exactly what's going on, you do two things: first, go home and get your Aunt Annie to give you breakfast, and, after you do that, go down to the clinic and have Dr. Coghill give you a checkup——"

"Aunt Annie isn't home, she's gone to Inverness to stay with her friend Ruby."

Nairne uttered an impatient exclamation. Of course, Annie had planned her little holiday to coincide with Kilty's trip on the *Bounty*. "And I suppose her place is locked up," she murmured, "but, even if you could have gotten in, you couldn't have stayed there on your own anyway..."

"Could I...stay here till she comes back?"

"Here?" Nairne raised her eyebrows, pausing with the coffee canister in one hand, the scoop in the other. "Well," she said after a moment, "I don't see why not. You could use one of the B and B rooms——"

"Could I sleep in the attic?"

"The attic? For heaven's sake, no, Kilty—you'd freeze to death up there."

"I didna last night."

His gray eyes had a mischievous, slightly cocky twinkle, and Nairne found herself laughing. "No, you didn't, did you?" She shrugged. "Okay," she said, "why not? But you'll have to fix up the mattress, and I'll give you some bedding and a lantern. Oh, and one rule..."

"Aye?"

"No smoking, Kilty." Her voice was firm. "If you want to smoke you'll have to go outside. I won't allow it in the house."

"Sure. No problem." Kilty hitched up his kilt, but as soon as he let go it slid back down his hips again at an angle. "I suppose I'll have to go back to school, now that I'm home."

"Yes," Nairne tried not to smile, "I suppose you will. But you'll have a bite to eat first. Here," she put a bowl and spoon on the table, "get some cereal from that cupboard—milk's in the fridge. Help yourself."

Now, she decided, was the time to ask him really why he had come back. "So tell me," she said casually as he poured milk on a heaping plate of cornflakes, "what made you decide to forgo the trip on the *Queen's Bounty*? I thought you were really looking forward to the experience."

Kilty pushed the milk jug into the center of the table, and bowed his head over his cereal. "I dinna want to talk about it, Nairne. It's...private."

Leaning back against the countertop, fingers curled around its smooth edge, Nairne looked at the boy with a mixture of frustration and compassion. He had been through more than a boy of fourteen should have to go through, and if he was having problems now they were problems he obviously didn't want to share with anyone. At least, not with her.

And she knew from experience when to push and when not to push. This was not a time for pushing.

"All right," she said gently. "But remember, if you do decide at any time that you'd like to talk, I'm here.

And anything you tell me will go no further, if that's the way you want it."

"Thanks, Nairne," he mumbled.

He'd wolfed down the cereal as if he hadn't eaten in a week. Now he pushed himself back from the table and got up. "Want these in the dishwasher?"

"No, in the sink, please. Kilty..."

"Aye?"

"About wiping out the message on my telephone answering machine——"

He sighed. "I'll work next weekend without pay."

"Good."

He straightened his shoulders. "Right, I'll be going, then."

"Should I make an appointment for you to see Dr. Coghill?" Nairne quirked a slightly mocking eyebrow.

He had the grace to blush. "No, I'll no' go to the doc—I'm sorry I lied to old Webster about that. I'm right as rain. I'm off to school now. See ye later."

Just as Kilty reached the door Strome Galbraith appeared in the doorway. As they passed each other Kilty flashed the dark stranger a quick, unreadable glance, and Strome's expression darkened. Nairne thought he was going to say something, but he just compressed his lips into a thin line and, with his gaze hooded, watched the boy leave.

A moment or two later the front door slammed shut. Nairne hadn't realized she'd been holding her breath till she heard it hiss out slowly. There, he was gone, thank goodness. When those two were together in the same room there was no mistaking the tension that twanged in the air between them. A tension that was as unsettling as it was mystifying. It must be something about their chemistry, she decided. What else could possibly cause the vibrations throbbing between them?

"All settled in?" she asked brightly as Strome came into the kitchen.

"Yes, thanks."

"Here, let me pour you a mug of coffee," she said. As she did she was aware that he had begun pacing restlessly up and down the kitchen, and once again she felt herself become uneasy. How different he was from Rory, she found herself reflecting; Rory had been so easygoing, so even-tempered. He had always accomplished whatever he'd set out to do, but had achieved his ends in a quietly methodical way without ever ruffling feathers or making enemies. It was a gift, she'd often told him.

And it was a gift that this Strome Galbraith obviously didn't possess. She could tell by the way he'd handled Kilty that he faced problems head-on and rode roughshod over anyone who got in his way.

She handed him the mug of coffee, but didn't bother inviting him to sit down; she sensed that he was far too restless to do so. She also sensed that he wanted to talk to her. But about what?

"Tell me," he said abruptly, "about that boy. What's his history?"

Well, surprise! She'd been bemoaning the fact just a short time ago that she'd lost his interest when she'd begun talking about the boys she worked with—now he was actually asking questions about one of them!

"Kilty?" Nairne poured herself a mug of coffee, and, adding milk and sugar, stirred it before making her way to the table. She sat down, hands cupped around the mug. "He's a nice kid——"

"Nice?" A disbelieving smile twisted Strome's lips. "I inferred from what you told me that the boys you work with are delinquents, and, from the little I've seen of this Somerled, or Kilty, or whatever the hell his name is——"

"First of all," Nairne forced herself to stay calm, "yes, the boys who work at Bruach have all been in trouble with the law—with the exception of Kilty. His story is different."

"In what way?"

"Kilty's younger than most of the lads, and he's been working here only since his father died." Nairne stared out of the window, absently noting that Kilty must have let Shadow out; the black collie was lying stretched out in the sun beside her van in the drive. "He's always been a loner—never was one of the crowd, as it were. He's an original——" Nairne gave a rueful laugh "—you've probably gathered that yourself, from the way he dresses——"

Strome grunted. "You're right about that. I can't imagine too many lads his age are comfortable wearing the kilt."

"When he was about three Hazel—his mother—started making him wear a kilt to Sunday school. The older kids used to tease him—they nicknamed him Kilty. He was never made to wear the kilt after he started going to Glencraig Primary, but the nickname stuck." Nairne placed her mug on the table, and thoughtfully ran a finger around the rim. "When he was twelve he went to a Boy Scout jamboree in Edinburgh. When Hazel and Hugh went to the train station to meet him they didn't recognize him. He'd traded his jeans for that Black Watch kilt—it hung way down below his knees in those days—and his hair was purple. The kilt has been his trade mark ever since."

There was a long silence in the kitchen, broken only by the sound of the Glencraig church clock in the distance as it rang out the hour. When the echoes faded away Strome placed his coffee mug on the countertop and moved across to the window. He leaned his shoulder against the wall, and, folding his arms, looked across at Nairne.

"You mentioned that his parents are dead. Who's looking after the lad now?"

How strange that he'd seem so interested in a boy who apparently rubbed him up the wrong way, and so intensely! "Kilty's only relative is Annie Low, an elderly aunt of Hugh's, and she became the boy's legal guardian after Hugh died.'' Nairne shook her head. ''Poor Annie, she's been a spinster all her days—hasn't the first idea how to cope with Kilty. And that's how I got involved,'' she went on. ''She asked me if I could give him an odd job now and again after school, so that I could keep an eye on him.''

''You appear to have a good relationship with the boy.'' Strome's blue eyes fixed Nairne steadily.

''I like him,'' she said. ''As I told you, he's a nice lad. But I am worried about him. Living with Annie, and working here for me, he doesn't have a male role model . . .''

''How does he get on at school?''

''Oh, he's smart as a whip but he doesn't apply himself. He has only one *real* interest in his life and that's——''

The ringing of the phone interrupted Nairne's words. With an ''Excuse me,'' she went to pick up the receiver.

''Nairne,'' Kyla's voice came across the line, ''I forgot to copy down that recipe we were talking about last night. Do you have time to give me it now?''

''Oh, sure—just a sec till I get my notebook.''

Nairne put down the receiver. ''I'm sorry,'' she glanced at Strome, ''I'll be on the phone for a few minutes. Will you be going out this morning?''

''Mm, I thought I'd . . . explore the place.''

Why would a city man want to putter around a small Scottish village in the bleakest of February weather when he could afford to fly to the Riviera, or Florida, or the Bahamas? Nairne found herself wondering. Ah, well, she reflected, to each his own.

''Normally, I offer my B and Bs only breakfast, and a cuppa in the evening,'' she said as she picked up her notebook and flipped through the pages. ''But, since you're on your own, and most of the touristy places are shut at this time of year, you're welcome to join me at mealtimes. Just let me know in advance if you're not going to be in.''

"Thanks. Today, then, I'll be out till around five."

Thank goodness, thought Nairne...and then, startled, wondered why that had been her immediate reaction. But of course she knew the answer to that! She'd never before met anyone who could unsettle her so, just by his presence. She had never before been so physically aware of a man—and it wasn't simply because of his looks, his black hair and intensely blue eyes. What was really disturbing her was something less tangible. It was his invisible magnetism that was reaching out to her, stimulating an almost painful yearning inside her, a yearning for——

Abruptly she slammed a gate across her recklessly straying thoughts.

"Fine," she said. Then, giving him what she hoped he would interpret as a dismissive nod, she crossed to the phone and picked it up again. As he touched the fingertips of his right hand to his forehead in a farewell salute his lips curved in a crooked smile that set Nairne's pulses fluttering in an erratic way that alarmed her. Lordy, she thought, fighting a feeling of panic, someone should lock this man up and throw away the key; he was a heartbreaker if ever she saw one!

It wasn't till she heard the front door shut behind him that she realized she'd been holding her breath. Letting it out in a shuddering rush, she picked up the handset.

"Are you still there, Kyla?"

"Are you all right, Nairne? You don't sound like yourself this morning."

She didn't feel like herself, either, Nairne thought a little wildly. "We must have a bad connection. I'm fine." But, even as she spoke the words, she noticed that her heartbeats were still hammering erratically. What on earth was happening to her?

The answer, of course, was there, somewhere in her head...but instead of trying to track it down she quickly diverted her brain from that task to the one on hand.

"Do you have a pen, Kyla? Right, here's the recipe."

"That's lovely, then." Her gruff uncle hung up.
Tansy, on the sofa, propped against the arm, picked
with idle sympathy and smart ...

CHAPTER FOUR

KILTY came home from school at four, and Nairne set
him immediately to fixing up the attic bedroom. He came
down shortly after, and assured Nairne there was no
danger of the bed's collapsing again.

"I've put two boards under the box spring," he explained, "so it's impossible for it to fall through. It's
actually more comfortable than the bed I have at
Annie's."

"Good." Nairne was standing at the sink peeling potatoes, and she paused for a moment, turning to him.
"By the way, I dropped by to see Annie one morning
last week, and she showed me the photographs you've
got pinned to one of the walls in your room. They're
absolutely wonderful."

"Thanks, Nairne."

There was, she noted, no false modesty in his reply.
And, apart from a faint hint of color tinging his high-
boned cheeks, no sign that her praise had affected him
in any way. And her praise had been genuine; the en-
larged photographs were scenes of Glencraig, the loch,
and the surrounding mountains, and they had been so
beautiful that she'd felt her breath catch in her throat
as she'd looked at them. "But Annie said," she went
on, "that you'd given up your photography since you
moved in with her. Why, Kilty?"

He shrugged, and his eyes slid away from hers. "Just
lost interest, I guess. Besides, you know how cramped
Annie's but 'n' ben is—there isn't even the tiniest corner
for me to have a darkroom. I packed all my things away."

"Your camera too?"

He shuffled his feet and screwed up his thin face in a
grimace. "I sold it."

Nairne couldn't hide her shock. "You sold it? Oh, Kilty, how *could* you? Your Mam told me how hard Hugh saved to buy you that Nikon—he made a lot of sacrifices to——"

Stunned, she watched as tears sprang to Kilty's eyes. With the back of his sleeve he brushed them roughly away, blindly pushing past her as he did. "I don't want to talk about it, Nairne," he said in a choked voice. "I've lost interest in photography—don't you understand? It was just a childish thing. I've gotten over it."

He pushed open the kitchen door and a moment later she heard his steps on the stair. Going up to the attic, she thought, going up to be alone. She felt her heart ache for him. There was more to his story than he had let on; something must have happened to make him give up his beloved photography. Something deeply personal, and something that appeared to have hurt him very much. What on earth could it have been? Oh, it wasn't just that Annie didn't have space for a darkroom. His dreams had been too strong for him to have allowed them to be snuffed out so easily——

The sound of the front door shutting made her start. That must be Strome, she thought—and he would be looking for his dinner. Quickly she set herself to finishing the potatoes, and was just peeling the last one when she heard his step in the hall.

A moment later he came through the doorway, his broad shoulders almost filling it. And as he moved forward Nairne couldn't help noticing that with him he brought an aura of energy and vitality.

"Something smells good," he said.

"Lentil soup." Nairne tumbled the potatoes into a pan of boiling water on the Aga, and said in a casual voice, "So where did you get to this afternoon?"

"Oh, here and there." He had come to a stop in the middle of the room and was standing there aimlessly.

Nairne recognized the signs of a male feeling out of his depth in a woman's domain, and she treated him the way she would have treated any one of the lads in her care. "Here, come and make yourself useful," she said, handing him a long-handled wooden spoon. "Give the soup a stir."

The soup didn't need stirring...but then he would never know that. She had found that when one of the boys came wandering into the kitchen and stood there, hovering, he usually wanted to be around a woman, but didn't know it. Just giving him something to do seemed to make him more comfortable. Would it work with this bleakly withdrawn man?

As he took the spoon from her she noticed that his breath was very faintly laced with alcohol.

"Ah," she smiled wryly, "you ended up at the Royal, talking with the locals."

He looked down at her, and for the first time she saw a smile in his eyes. "Guilty, m'lady."

He was standing much closer than she had meant him to when she had handed him the spoon. And now she not only smelled the hint of alcohol, but she also smelled the male scent of his body. She found it disturbing. And because she found it disturbing she moved back a little, and steered the conversation in a direction she knew she could handle. "Rory used to do that sometimes, go in past the Royal on his way home if he'd been down at the station sending the veg off to London on the afternoon train." There, she thought, that felt better, as if she had placed Rory right there between them, to block off the sexual vibrations that tingled between her and this stranger. "You're a dab hand at the soup stirring," she said lightly as she continued peeling the last potato. "You must have had a few lessons in your day! Are you married?"

Damned fool! she chastised herself swiftly and mercilessly. After what he'd insinuated last night, had she now put herself in a position where he'd interpret her question as being asked for the specific purpose of finding out whether or not he was fancy-free?

But, to her relief, he treated her question as lightly as she'd asked it. "No," he said, giving the soup a swirl with the wooden spoon, "I'm not married, haven't ever been married... nor am I ever likely to be married. I'm afraid I'd be a poor candidate for that sacred institution."

"And why would that be?"

"Because every time the poor woman would be out of my sight," he retorted, "I'd be thinking she was going to meet a lover. And what kind of basis would that be for a happy marriage?"

"You're the jealous type?" Nairne's tone was frankly disbelieving. "Sorry, I don't buy it."

"No, not the jealous type. The cynical type."

"Cynical? As in...?"

"As in I've never met a woman yet whom I could trust."

So that explained it. The man had obviously had a bad experience with a woman. Probably more than one, if the hard cynicism of his expression was anything to go by. And was that why he had looked the way he had when he'd watched the happy scene with Kyla and family in her living room the previous evening?

"You're not leaping to defend your sex?" His tone was gently mocking.

"No." Nairne looked up at him with a level gaze. "I'm afraid I can't speak for anyone but myself in that regard. But I'm sorry that you've had bad luck——"

"Bad luck?" His laugh was contemptuous. "Luck had nothing to do with it. The woman I was involved with was hard, manipulative and two-timing. In short, an absolute bitch——"

"Nairne."

Nairne swiveled around as she heard Kilty's voice behind her. He was standing in the doorway, and when her quick glance encompassed his pale face and tightly drawn features she felt dismay sweep through her. He was looking not at her but at Strome, staring at him, and his eyes held an alarming mixture of anger, confusion and utter misery.

Involuntarily she took a couple of steps toward him, but he in turn stepped back, so that he was out in the lobby again. "I'm off out," he said in a choking voice. "I've done my homework. I'll be back by ten."

"Kilty——"

But before Nairne could stop him he was gone. Down the lobby, across the hall and out of the front door, smashing it shut with a force that reverberated through the whole house. What in heaven's name, she wondered fearfully, was the matter with him? She'd never seen him act so strangely. It had nothing to do with her, she was sure of that. Therefore, it had to do with Strome Galbraith.

But he'd never met the man before today.

What in heaven's name could the stranger have done to upset the boy so? He had, of course, been the one to find Kilty sneaking from the house that morning, but Kilty had been well aware he'd been in the wrong, and, besides, she knew he wasn't one to bear a grudge. No, there had to be something else.

The simplest thing to do, of course, would be to come right out and ask Strome what he had done to cause such a reaction, but her deepest instincts told her that, whatever was going on between the two, it was something neither of them was about to share with her.

She sighed as she turned back into the kitchen again. With most of the lads who had worked at Bruach during the past eight years she had eventually managed to build a good relationship, and had never made the mistake of allowing herself to become emotionally involved. With Kilty it was different—she was very attached to the boy. Probably, of course, because she and Hazel had been such close friends, and she'd known Kilty since the day he was born——

"A penny for them."

"Oh...I was just thinking," she walked across to the Aga, "about the day Kilty was born." She pulled the pan of potatoes to the side and the rolling boil settled to a simmer. "He was born a month early, but even so he weighed more than eight pounds. And a roaring, lusty baby he was—I remember Hughie saying, 'Well, he came in like a lion, didn't he?' You see, he was born on the first of March! His birthday will be coming up soon..."

"And he's going to be...?"

"Fifteen. He looks older, because he's tall, and well-built."

"And you say he was...premature?"

"Mm. Hugh had been away fishing for a couple of months, and he and Hazel were married shortly after he came back. Annie was the midwife who delivered him. I remember her trying to insist it was a full-term baby, but she was getting on—Kilty was actually the very last baby she delivered—and, of course, she was wrong. It couldn't have been a full-term baby because Hugh had been away at the fishing for all of May and the best part of June..."

"You mean," Strome said with an ironic twist of his lips, "if the baby *had* been full-term, Hugh couldn't have been the father."

"That's right." Nairne absently took some cutlery from a drawer and began setting the table. "And of course there was no question of that."

"Why not?"

Something in Strome's voice, a quiet coldness, sent a shiver through Nairne. Blinking, she looked up at him, and was surprised to see the hard, scornful look in his eyes.

"Why not?" she asked, and heard a faint defensiveness in her tone. "Because Hazel wasn't that kind of girl! She and Hugh had been going together since they were in school. She was promised to him."

"Promised to him?"

"That's right."

"They weren't engaged, though."

"No," Nairne said evenly. "They weren't engaged. Hazel didn't have a ring, but everybody knew that it was only a matter of time before they got married." Why on earth was he so interested in Kilty? she wondered. And why so interested in Hazel? A fleeting memory of the first time she'd seen him darted into her mind, a picture of him standing staring at Hazel's grave. She had thought she'd heard him say something, and when she'd approached him the expression on his face had been bleak, and bitter, and something else, which she hadn't recognized then, but recognized now as she saw the same look in his eyes. A contemptuous look.

But when she'd asked him then if he'd known Hazel he had denied it.

No, she corrected herself, he hadn't actually denied it, had he? What he *had* done was change the subject, and very neatly. He had shrugged, and said he was just interested in old graveyards.

Nairne felt her heart give a jarring shudder as the truth suddenly hit her.

This man had known Hazel.

Or at the very least had known *of* her. And, for some reason, had hated her.

Nairne felt as if someone had hit her on the head and stunned her; what ghost from the past haunted this enigmatic stranger? And why, if it caused him so much pain, had he come back to expose himself to it?

Hardly knowing what she was doing, she took a fork from the drawer and tested the potatoes. They were ready. With a murmured "Excuse me," she passed in front of Strome on her way to the sink to strain the vegetables.

She didn't know why he had come to Glencraig. She couldn't even make a guess. But already his presence was causing a disturbance. It was like a stone thrown carefully into the middle of a peaceful pool; no matter how smooth the stone, no matter how peaceful the pool, ripples were going to be made, and the pool wouldn't be peaceful and smooth again till the last ripple had disappeared.

Or, in this case, till Strome Galbraith had gone home.

No sooner had the thought occurred to her than she followed it up, as if by talking about it she could make him disappear.

"Where do you come from, Mr. Galbraith?"

"London. I have a apartment in the city."

"What kind of business are you in?" Nairne filled the kettle with cold water and plugged it in as she spoke.

"Construction."

"You're in the housing business . . . or is it commercial construction?" She reached for the multicolored cotton napkins nestled in a basket on the countertop.

"I build lodges around the world—for sports enthusiasts. Mainly mountaineers," he added. "Crest Construction——"

"Crest Construction?" Nairne paused, the napkins in her hands forgotten for the moment. "*Crest* Construction? Why, they own the property adjacent to Bruach . . . about a hundred acres in all." She stared at him. "*You* own it? *You* are Crest Construction?"

"That's right, Mrs. Campbell——"

"Oh, do for heaven's sake stop calling me Mrs. Campbell," she said distractedly. "Everybody calls me Nairne. Mr. Galbraith——"

"Strome," he interrupted mockingly.

"Strome——" Nairne waved a dismissive hand "—why have you been holding on to that property? The land has been lying fallow for . . . oh, it must be fifteen years."

"And why would that interest you?" he asked, his dark brows quirked derisively.

Nairne took in a deep breath. "Because Rory and I tried to buy five acres of it a few years ago, through our lawyer, but the lawyer at Crest Construction—*your* lawyer—told us it was not for sale.''

''*You* wanted to buy part of Craigend? Not for the old farmhouse, obviously—it's just a pile of rocks and a moldering thatched roof!''

''No, not for the farmhouse—it's an eyesore and should be torn down and carted away. The site, though, is wonderful—there's a view right down the glen, and over the loch. No, it was just the land we wanted.''

''And what did you plan to do with it?''

''We were going to devote an area by the road to a youth center for teenagers, and the rest we planned to put into raspberries.''

''Ah.''

''And you,'' she said quietly, ''what did you plan to do with it, at the time you purchased it? For I'm sure an obviously successful businessman like yourself wouldn't have bought property without having had some purpose in mind for it.''

''I planned, at that time, to construct a mountain-eering lodge.''

''A mountaineering lodge! Right next to Bruach?'' Nairne frowned a little as she turned the idea over in her mind.

''Do I detect . . . disapproval . . . in your reaction?'' he interrupted her thoughts.

Nairne paused for a few moments before answering, and when she spoke it was slowly, consideringly. ''No, I think it would have been good for Glencraig, in many ways. It would have brought lots of work, at a time when jobs had become very scarce . . . as they still are. But . . .''

''Ah, yes, there's always a but . . .''

''Well, I would hate to see a modern, glitzy type of place—I would hate to see Glencraig spoiled.''

''I don't spoil things, Nairne.''

The words were spoken simply, but firmly. And they made her glance up into his eyes. He was looking down at her, and for the very first time that she could recall, his eyes were clear and direct. "I don't spoil things," he repeated, this time more softly, and Nairne felt her breath catch in her throat as his gaze flickered over her face, lingering at her mouth, which all of a sudden seemed dry and parched. Involuntarily she moistened the flesh of her lower lip with the tip of her tongue...and as she did she saw his eyes darken.

"Especially," he murmured huskily, "things that are beautiful."

She knew he was going to kiss her, but she couldn't move. And it wasn't just because he had shifted slightly and she was trapped between him and the countertop, it was because a surge of desire had drained every ounce of strength from her body. He wasn't even touching her, but she felt her heart fluttering in her throat as she watched him bend his head, saw his eyelids begin to close, saw his lips move slightly as they aimed unerringly for hers...

Yearning, aching, for his kiss, she closed her eyes and tilted her face up to him——

The doorbell rang when their lips were so close that she could feel their heat against her skin. With a gulp, a squeaky, "Oh, let me by, there's someone at the door," she somehow managed to duck away from him. She didn't turn and look back as she fled across the kitchen. All she wanted to do was get away from him before she was foolish enough to do something she would regret.

Raking a hand through her hair to tidy it, she stood for a moment inside the front door, trying to catch her breath. How could she have allowed herself to get trapped in such a situation, she wondered despairingly...and, worse, how could she have reacted the way she had to his closeness? For there was no doubt in her mind that, had the doorbell not rung, she would have given herself eagerly to his kiss.

She fought back a little moan, a moan that was drowned out by the sound of the bell as it rang again.

Swallowing hard, she forced her features into an artificially calm mask, and opened the door.

"Ah, Nairne," the thin, sandy-haired man standing on the top step smiled in greeting, "I'm glad you're home."

"Dr. Coghill! How nice to see you. Do come in." Nairne stepped aside and ushered him into the hall. What on earth could he want? She hadn't sent for him...had he somehow sensed that she needed him? That she had come down suddenly, unexpectedly with some nameless illness, that she was suffering from a restless fever of the blood? Stifling a hysterical laugh, she said, "Would you like me to take your coat?"

"Thanks." He shrugged off his sheepskin jacket, and waited while she hung it in the cupboard.

"Let's go into the living room." She led the way, and took advantage of the opportunity to get her rapid breathing back to normal...and her thoughts away from the disturbing man in the kitchen.

"Now," she said after they had sat down, one at either side of the hearth where the embers of a fire glowed, "how can I help you?"

"I've just had a call from Inverness, from Annie Low," he said. "She's had a wee turn and was taken into Raigmore Hospital——"

"Oh, I'm so sorry!" Nairne sat forward anxiously. "Is she going to be all right?"

"Aye, she's going to be all right. But I'm afraid she won't be coming back to her own place in Glencraig. I had a talk with the doctor involved in her case, and he says she'll no longer be able to look after herself. He's going to keep her at Raigmore for several days, give her a complete rest, and then he's going to arrange for her to be taken back here by ambulance to the Craigie Home for Seniors. You know, of course, that she should have been there years ago—the woman's close to ninety!"

"Didn't she apply for a room at the home last year? As I remember, she got one."

"Aye, but, after Hazel and Hugh were gone and she had Kilty to think of, she turned it down. I tried to talk her out of it at the time, but didn't get to first base. The alternative, of course, was to have put Kilty into a foster home and she just wouldn't hear of it. Of course, looking after a teenage boy at her age was far too much for her."

"Of course, and the Craigie Home will be the best place for her. But what's going to happen to Kilty now? He doesn't have anyone. Oh, I wish I could help in some way."

The doctor cleared his throat. "Nairne, I have an idea—now, I don't want you to give me an answer right away, because I know it's something that will require a great deal of thought on your part...but..."

He hesitated, and Nairne, wondering what on earth he was going to ask her, urged him to go on. "You know I'll do anything I can for Kilty. He's a grand lad, one of the best."

The doctor stood up, and, ramming his hands into the pockets of his baggy blue cords, subjected Nairne to a long and steady look from behind his gold-rimmed glasses. Then she saw his lips move in a little smile. "Nairne, lass," he said softly, "I know just how lonely you've been since Rory died. And, though I know how busy you've kept yourself, and I know how good your parents and Kyla and Adam have been to you, it's not quite the same as having someone of your own. What I'm trying to say...and not making a very good job of it...is this. Would ye consider adopting the lad?"

Nairne paced the living room at five to ten, waiting for Kilty to come in. For the twentieth time she glanced at the carriage clock on the mantelpiece. Dr. Coghill had left her to tell Kilty what had happened to his great-aunt, and when she had explained that the boy was already staying at Bruach they had agreed the best thing to do at present was to let him stay on there till a decision was made.

And what was she going to decide? Nairne wondered restlessly as she crossed to the large window. Pulling back the heavy rose curtain, she stared out into the dark.

Ever since Dr. Coghill had made his suggestion she had been unable to think of anything else. She had gone back to the kitchen, and chatted abstractedly while she and Strome Galbraith had eaten dinner. She knew he must have thought her withdrawn manner was due to their near kiss earlier, but in truth she just hadn't given it any more thought. And she had been thankful when, after a second cup of coffee, he'd risen from the table and said he was going out for a walk.

Questions that had niggled at her earlier—why was the man in Glencraig, what connection did he have with Hazel, why wasn't he interested in selling Craigend?— had faded away into insignificance as she focused her mind solely on the doctor's suggestion.

The sound of the front door opening, and closing again, had her heartbeats skittering nervously. She crossed swiftly to the living room door and opened it...and saw, as she had expected, that it was Kilty.

"Come on in," she said with a smile. "I've been waiting for you."

"I'm not late, Nairne, am I?" He was wearing no jacket over his black T-shirt, and yet he didn't appear to be feeling the cold. He bent to take off his Reeboks, and as he walked past her into the living room his white-socked feet made no sound on the floor. There was, she noticed, a smell of tobacco lingering around him.

"Would you like a glass of milk?" she offered.

"No, thanks. I just had a Coke."

As Nairne perched on the arm of the sofa he dropped into one of the armchairs, sitting forward with his legs out straight in front of him, his kilt draped over his knees, his hands on his thighs. "Did you want to talk to me about something?"

"Yes." No point in beating around the bush, Nairne decided as she met his frank, intelligent gaze. Best tell him the worst and get it over with. "Dr. Coghill called around at dinnertime. Your Aunt Annie had a turn, and was taken to Raigmore——"

Kilty got to his feet with a jerky movement. "Is she going to be all right?" His Adam's apple twitched, and color flushed up into his cheeks. "Can we go and see her?"

"She's going to be fine." Nairne's voice was as reassuring as she could make it, "but we won't get to see her for several days. She's to have a complete rest. Then they're going to bring her back by ambulance..."

"I'll have to go around to her place before then—I'll have to make sure everything's ready for her coming back. I'll have to get some bread and milk in and——"

"Kilty, you won't be looking after her. She's being taken to Craigie Home."

There was a long silence as the boy assimilated the information Nairne had given him. Then just as she was about to speak again she saw his stiff shoulders relax a little, and he said quietly, "That's good—that she's got a place at the Craigie Home." He looked into the embers of the fire and Nairne could see tears glimmering in his eyes. "It was too much for her, looking after me. But she just wouldna listen. Now she'll have someone looking after her."

Nairne felt her heart clench with emotion. He obviously hadn't given a thought to his own predicament—to the fact that the change in his great-aunt's situation meant that there would have to be a change in his own. A change that could lead to another drastic upheaval in his life.

And as she looked at him, at the bravado expressed in his outlandish way of dressing, and at the childish vulnerability of his young face, which showed clear signs of the pain he'd known in his life, she knew what she had to do.

Knew what she wanted to do.

And as she made her decision she felt as if a heavy burden was lifting from her heart, and it seemed to be weightless, as it hadn't been for many months.

She stood up and clasped her hands tightly together as she looked at him. To her surprise, her palms were slick with perspiration. But why wouldn't they be? she asked herself. It wasn't every day that a woman made such a momentous decision.

But what would Kilty's reaction be?

"I think I'll go to bed, Nairne." He hitched up his kilt, but it immediately slid back down over his hips again. "By the way, I've made up my mind to stop smoking. I know you don't like it, and I don't want you worrying about me setting Bruach on fire. I had my last one outside just now."

"What would you think about staying on here, Kilty?" As soon as the words were out, Nairne felt the boy become tense again. "And I don't mean up in the attic, although that's okay temporarily, if that's what you want. No, I mean to live here at Bruach, now that Annie's going to be at the Craigie Home."

"You mean...permanently?" Kilty's gray eyes were guarded. "Like...one of your B and Bs?"

Nairne's laugh was shaky. "No, silly..." Oh, Lord, she shouldn't have laughed. The boy's eyes had become shuttered, his body even stiffer. He thought he'd somehow made a fool of himself, been presumptuous. Quickly she went on, "Dr. Coghill thought it might be a good idea if I were to...adopt you. Rather than have you sent to a foster home, you could live with me. We'd do it formally, so it would all be legal..."

He bent down and began adjusting the cuff of one of his socks...but, though he had moved quickly, he hadn't moved quickly enough. Nairne had seen the shine in his eyes, and it was no surprise to her when he brushed the back of his sleeve across them before he straightened.

"You've thought about it, Nairne?" he said gruffly. "It's what you really want?"

"Yes," she said with a smile. And she knew beyond a shadow of a doubt that she'd made the right decision. "Do you think we could make a go of it?"

Before he could answer the sound of the front door opening broke into the tentative emotion dancing between them. She saw his eyes cloud, saw him straighten his shoulders. What awful timing, Nairne thought frustratedly. Why couldn't Strome Galbraith have stayed out ten minutes longer? Perhaps he'll go straight upstairs...

But he didn't. As she and Kilty stood there, waiting, listening, the door of the living room opened, and Strome came into the room. He seemed quite unaware of any tension in the atmosphere, and, walking over to the fire, held out his hands to the glow. "Cold night," he muttered. "Damned cold, even for February."

"I'm off to bed, Nairne. Thanks for telling me about Annie. When she's well enough for visitors I'll go and see her." He let his gaze dart briefly toward Strome before turning again to Nairne. "As for what we were talking about, I think it's a great idea. And I don't have any other choice, do I? With my Mam and Dad dead, and Annie going into a home, I don't have a living relative to look after me. I'd be proud to have you adopt me."

For the first time ever he hugged Nairne. It was a fleeting, awkward embrace, and she was conscious only of the grape scent from his purple hair gel, and the tobacco smell from his T-shirt, and then he was gone. But his youth and his vulnerability melted her heart.

It was going to work, she knew, because they both wanted it to.

She couldn't wait to tell Kyla!

In the meantime, she decided as the living room door closed and she was left alone with Strome Galbraith, she simply had to share her news with someone, and celebrate. It wasn't every day she found out she was going to become a mother!

"Will you join me in a glass of Scotch?" She turned to him cheerfully. "Such a lot has happened tonight——"

"I heard," he said in a grating voice. His eyes were so dark and haunted that Nairne felt a shiver run down her spine. "You're going to adopt the boy. Do you think that's a wise decision?"

For a moment she could say nothing, so stunned was she by his attitude. Then she said firmly, "Yes, I'm sure it's a wise decision. Kilty needs me... and I need him... and we're both strong enough to admit it. No man is an island, Strome. I'm sure that saying is familiar to you." She inhaled a deep breath. She had told herself several times that, whatever problem Strome Galbraith had, it was none of her business, and she shouldn't poke her nose in where it quite obviously wasn't wanted. But something inside her, something she couldn't control, was pushing her, driving her, to try to help this man. Crossing to the fire, she took a crisp, dry log from the log box, and placed it atop the softly glowing embers in the fire. Then, dusting her palms on the seat of her jeans, she straightened and faced him again.

"Haven't you ever known what it's like to need someone?" she asked softly. "Or are you made of stone?"

CHAPTER FIVE

IF NAIRNE had thought her straightforward attack would disconcert Strome, she was mistaken. She might have expected him to react by withdrawing, or by himself attacking...but what he did was neither. He laughed at her. The laugh was tinged with mockery, but it was a laugh nevertheless, and there was even a glint of dry humor in his blue eyes.

"Oh, I have needs, Nairne, just like the next man. The basic needs of life—hunger, thirst, and the safety needs——"

"And, I'm sure, the need for belonging and the need for love—though you apparently would wish to deny those particular needs." Nairne crossed to a carved-oak bureau and lowered the hinged lid, revealing a sparsely furnished cocktail tray. Pouring a dram into each of two heavy crystal glasses, she asked, "How do you like your Scotch?"

"Straight," he said, walking over to join her. He took the glass in one of his lean, well-shaped hands and, walking back across to the hearth, leaned against the wall by the mantelpiece. "So," he drawled, "belonging and love. Let's take belonging first. Are we talking here about belonging to a place...or belonging to a person?"

Nairne closed the lid of the bureau. "Both, I think. When I say 'I belong to Glencraig,' I mean that I live here, and I've always lived here, and so I'm part of it, and it's part of me." She crossed over to the sofa, and, sinking down on the center cushion, looked up at Strome. "And you—do you, in the same way, belong to London?"

His shrug was careless. "No," he said, "I don't, as you put it, belong to London. I was born in Manchester,

I've traveled all over the world, and I live in London because my office is in London... but for me home is wherever I am at the moment."

"But that's not 'home.'" Nairne sipped from her glass. "You're going to stay here for a few days, but this isn't your home! How can you say it is?"

"The point I'm trying to make is that I have no home. I don't belong anywhere. For me, it's not a need."

"But your place in London——"

"A base. A place to hang my hat."

"Tell me about it."

He gulped down a mouthful of his drink. "What do you want to know? It's a penthouse apartment, with a view over the city—it has three bedrooms, a living room, a dining room, and an electronic kitchen that looks like something out of a spaceship. Oh, and it also has two bathrooms and a darkroom."

"A darkroom? You're interested in photography?"

"Let's say... it used to be one of my main interests."

"And were you good at it?"

"Good enough to make a living at it."

"Oh, but that's so interesting! I do admire people who have the gift of looking through a camera lens and seeing more than the average person sees. My own photography skills," she added with a rueful chuckle, "extend no further than being able not to cut people's feet off. Most of the time, that is..."

"You have, I'm sure, other talents."

"No," Nairne smiled up at him, "I'm afraid I haven't. I'm really very ordinary. I do come from a very talented and creative family, though. My mother, Kate, is a wonderful artist, my father, Mac, is an inventor, and my sister, Kyla—of course, you've met Kyla! Isn't she beautiful? She has inherited Kate's artistic talent—she did that lovely watercolor on your bedroom wall. Did you notice it?"

"Yes, I noticed it—a stand of birch trees above the distillery. It's very good." His tone was absent, as if he was thinking about something else. "Ordinary." He shook his head, looking down at her with a strange, indecipherable expression in his blue gaze. "How can you possibly think of yourself as ordinary? You're the least ordinary-looking woman I've ever seen."

Laughter twinkled in Nairne's eyes as they met his. "Oh, I wasn't talking about looks," she retorted. "I know my looks aren't ordinary." She put down her glass and grasped a handful of the thick, shiny hair tumbling over her shoulders. "How could anyone with hair this dreadful color be described as ordinary? You don't have to tell me I stand out in a crowd. *That* I've known since I was old enough to look in a mirror. The only blessing," she added with a self-deprecatory grimace, "was that for some reason no one ever gave me a nickname. I spent my school years just dreading the day when someone would start calling me 'Carrots' or 'Red'!"

"My goodness, I don't believe it." Strome placed his glass on the mantelpiece with a thump and pushed himself away from the wall. "Here——" imperiously he held out a hand "—get up. I want to show you something."

Nairne hesitated, her eyes drawn magnetically to his long, well-shaped fingers. "What?" she asked tentatively.

"Up." It was a command.

And, for some reason Nairne couldn't fathom, one she couldn't disobey.

His grip was firm, and powerful, and the physical contact sent a surge of warmth through Nairne's body, followed immediately by an all-encompassing shiver... As if, she decided as she got unsteadily to her feet, she were coming down with some debilitating flu. Fighting a sudden constriction of her throat muscles, she made to pull her fingers from his, but his grasp only tightened.

"Over here," he said.

"Where?" she asked faintly, but he didn't answer, and only when he had guided her firmly across to the bureau, and she caught sight of his reflection in the large mirror hanging on the wall above it, did she understand what he was going to do.

He released her hand with an abrupt gesture, but, even as she hugged her arms around her waist, assailed suddenly by nerves, he moved behind her, and, grasping her shoulders with hard fingers, turned her so that she was looking directly into the silvered glass.

"There," he said, "look at that hair. *Dreadful*? Good heavens, woman, are you blind? *Color* blind? Your hair is glorious! I've never seen anything like it. The women I know in London would kill to find a hairdresser who could make their hair look like yours——"

"It's not out of a bottle!" Nairne broke in, her tone outraged. Her hair might not be a color she liked, but that color was her own!

"Of course it's not out of a bottle." Strome's voice was gently chiding. "You really are very dense! You admit your looks aren't ordinary, but you really haven't the faintest idea how very extraordinary they are, have you?" He gave her shoulders a little shake. "Look at yourself, will you? Tell me what you see!"

What did she see? She saw a woman she almost didn't recognize. It was so long since she'd seen her eyes sparkle with suppressed excitement the way they were doing now, so long since she'd seen her pale cheeks glow that way— so long since she'd seen her lips, now slightly parted, look so full, so dewy...so expectant——

She tightened them and took in a deep breath. "What do I see?" To her relief, her voice was quite steady. "I see a woman who's going to be thirty on her next birthday, a woman who looks every day her age, a woman with brash red hair, pale skin, and blue eyes." She lifted her shoulders in an attempt to communicate to him that she wanted him to release her from his grasp; he did...but only so that he could weave his fingers through the long curls cascading down her back.

"How strange," he murmured, his breath riffling the hair at her crown, "we seem to be seeing two entirely different people. I see a woman with a perfect oval face, skin like cream silk, a delightful nose with a scattering of... let me count them ... exactly five freckles, eyes as velvety blue as violets, and hair..." she felt her breath catch in her throat as he lifted her hair and buried his face in it, inhaling deeply as he did so "...hair that looks like gold coins tumbling in a waterfall of sunshine, hair that has the exquisite fragrance of wildflowers trembling in a summer breeze."

Nairne wanted to move away from him but she was powerless. And when he turned her around to face him she thought she was going to stop breathing. She was wearing an angora sweater, and she could feel his hands moving across its soft surface as he caressed her back. "Why," she murmured weakly, "who would have guessed that behind those cynical blue eyes lurked the soul of a poet? You'll have a hard time convincing me now that you're a man of stone——"

His lips blotted out whatever else she had been about to say, and she acknowledged, even as she clutched his shoulders for support, that whatever she had been about to say would have been so much mindless drivel. This man had mesmerized her——

Was it possible that he had even *hypnotized* her? While he had been waxing so poetic over what he considered her glorious beauty, had he actually stolen into her mind and captured it—with the same ease as he had just captured her lips?

"Sweet," he murmured, pulling her closer so that she felt his muscular thighs pressing against her softer contours, felt her breasts crushed gently against the hard wall of his chest. He obviously hadn't shaved since early morning, and Nairne felt the slight abrasion of his skin against her cheek as his lips traveled questingly along the delicate line of her jaw, finally nestling in a sensitive spot just below her ear. She could feel the heat of his breath against her nerve endings, could feel a tingling response shiver through her body. A response such as she'd never felt before. It was wild, and it was fierce, it was shattering. There was a chemistry sizzling between herself and this man, a chemistry that sucked the breath from her lungs and made her body feel as if it was on fire. Desire, shocking, terrifying in its raw power, shafted through her like a searing, blazing fire. As if from a great distance, she heard Strome's husky "Oh, my God!" and at the same time was aware of the convulsive tightening of his arms around her... aware of the intimacy of the embrace in which they were now locked, their bodies so close that he must be as aware of the swelling of her breasts as she was of the surging evidence that he was equally aroused.

The lips which had been so softly, skillfully teasing the delicate skin at her throat now returned with urgent speed to seek her own, which were parted helplessly. Warm, moist, sensual, this time they moved hungrily on hers, greedily, searchingly, as if this was a kiss he'd long been dreaming of, long been yearning for...

All her inhibitions had disappeared. She didn't stop to wonder why; all she could think of was assuaging this reckless hunger in her, a hunger that was as alien to her as were the erotic sensations tantalizing her nipples, the erotic sensations twisting and torturing the nerves deep in the hidden, most secret areas of her womanhood...

She was hardly aware of what was happening as they moved, still clinging desperately to each other, over to the long, cushioned sofa. Did she pull him down beside her... or had he been the one to take the initiative? Nairne didn't know; all she knew was that they were lying together, she on her back, her head supported by a plump satin cushion, he alongside, with one foot still on the floor, and his other leg thrown possessively across hers.

Eyes wide, she looked up into his as he gazed down at her passionately. His hands were sliding over her green button-up sweater, down to the hem, lifting it up, so that she felt the soft folds over her collarbone. Then his palms were rubbing over her breasts, over the tight little buds that had formed earlier, the tight little buds that were waiting to flower under his teasing touch. His thumbs were gentle as he ran them over the tips, over and over the tips, till Nairne thought she would die with the sheer, anguished ecstasy of it. And all the time his eyes held hers, the sharp blue gone, now smoky, almost gray, with the desire flooding through them. The skin over his cheekbones was taut, his black hair had fallen over his brow, his lips were parted...

The words he was whispering inflamed her so that she writhed under him, and a flare of heat sizzled through her as she saw his dark eyelashes flicker, saw his look become glazed, unfocused. Involuntarily, dreamily, she pushed back his disheveled hair with fingers that trembled. His brow felt clammy with sweat. Nairne found herself running her tongue over her lips, which suddenly seemed parched.

And as he began to fumble with the clasp of her bra she felt her heartbeats begin an almost frightening drumming against her rib cage. She should be stopping him, she knew, but she couldn't. She was a captive of her desire, enslaved by it, bound by the sexual magnetism of this man, this man who was drawing from her feelings she had never known existed——

Guilt cut through her like a red-hot knife. A cry of sorrow, a silent cry, was torn from her heart. Oh, dear lord, how could she? Was she really doing this? Was she really surrendering to the raw animal desire she felt for this man?

For this *stranger*?

This stranger who had just succeeded in opening her bra, and was sliding his palms over her naked ribs, with sensual abandon, his thumbs teasing the lower swells of her breasts, till she could scarcely breathe. Her head was tilted back, his lips were at her throat, skimming over her heated skin, nibbling at the sensitive flesh, working

their way down over her collarbone as he one by one
undid the small buttons of her sweater——

With a small moan she thrust her hands against his
chest and pushed upward as hard as she could. Even as
she did, she was aware of the drumming of his heartbeats against her palms, a fierce drumming, a passionate
drumming—a drumming that echoed the wild drumming
of her own heart.

"Stop," she gasped, her tone pleading, "I want to get
up."

For a moment she thought he was going to disregard
her command, wondered actually if he had even heard
it. He was kissing her cheek, his lips teasing their way
along her flushed skin on their journey back to her
mouth, and then, all of a sudden as if there had been
some time delay in his understanding of what she'd said,
he froze. Only for a moment. Then he uttered a low,
intense oath, and after that he inhaled a frustrated
breath, and then, and only then, did she feel his weight
lift from her body.

No point, she decided tremulously, in trying to fasten
the clasp of her bra with him watching, though she was
uncomfortable with it lying loose over her swollen
breasts, and she was intensely aware of the peaking of
her hardened nipples against the fine wool of her green
sweater; she did, though, fasten the buttons he'd slid
open, but before she could tidy the garment by pulling
it down over her hips she felt the brush of Strome's long
fingers against her own as he pulled the angora garment
tidily into place.

Twisting away from him, but still feeling her skin
tingling where he'd touched her, she stumbled to her feet
and moved behind the coffee table, as if it could
somehow help shield her from him. Her back was to the
fire, and she could feel the warmth of the glowing embers
on the backs of her legs, through her jeans. Folding her
arms over her breasts in a defensive gesture, she dropped
her eyelids and let her gaze fall to the carpet, well aware

of the picture she must present, her cheeks pink, her lips trembling, her hair tumbling in wild dishevelment around her shoulders.

She had expected him to break the silence, to say something that would in all likelihood be accusing and hurtful, but when he didn't speak, finally, with a great effort she dragged her gaze up and looked at him.

With a sense of shock she saw he was sitting back comfortably, one leg casually draped over the other at the knee, one arm thrown carelessly along the back of the sofa. He looked as cool, Nairne thought with amazement, as if they had just been discussing the price of cabbages, instead of being on the point of consummating their brief two-day acquaintance with a frantic and shameless sexual union on the chintz-covered couch she and Rory had bought the week before their wedding...

Guilt shafted through her again, making her feel as if her heart had turned into a leaden weight in her chest. All because of this man. And she could tell by the way he was looking up at her, one dark eyebrow quirked, that he expected *her* to be the one to open the conversation. And, of course, she had to admit that, since she was the one who had broken away, the onus was on her to say something.

But what?

She cleared her throat. "Well——" Her voice was little more than a squeak. She cleared her throat again, this time with more force, and ran the tip of her tongue over her upper lip before repeating, "Well," and then adding in a voice that was little more than a whisper, "that was...unexpected."

Strome's other eyebrow shot up to quirk alongside its mate. "Unexpected?" His chuckle came from somewhere deep in his throat. "Oh, Nairne, who are you trying to fool? Yourself? It might have been many things, but unexpected was not one of them. Delightful, exciting...and in the end exquisitely frustrating. But unexpected...no.''

''Well,'' she retorted with a stubborn lift of her chin, ''I say it *was*!''

He laughed as if he found her denial extremely amusing. ''You can *say* it was if you wish, but saying it won't make it so. You know as well as I do that it was only a matter of time before we kissed.''

In the deepest recesses of her soul she knew he was right. She had never let the idea surface, it had been too frightening, too unthinkable...but the idea had been there, nevertheless. It had been there ever since the first spark of electricity had sizzled between them.

For the third time she felt guilt surge painfully through her. Guilt so strong that it made her react to Strome's gentle arrogance with an uncharacteristic haughtiness. ''You're very presumptuous.'' She tried to smooth her hair, but she felt it bounce back jauntily under her palms, and with an impatient exclamation she began toying with her gold wedding band.

''No,'' he said with a small shake of his head, ''I don't think so. Though I do admit I was wrong about one thing——''

''You do?'' she asked with a cold glare. ''And what was that?''

''The first night when you came along to my room——''

''You accused me of wanting to go to bed with you!'' Nairne tossed her hair back. ''I did not!''

''No, you didn't, did you? Not then.'' His dark eyes held a mocking gleam. ''But...you do now.''

Nairne felt her breath catch in her throat. What was happening to her? With an effort she quelled the panic that was making her heartbeats rush along so frighteningly. She had to put a stop to whatever it was this man was doing to her. And she had to put a stop to it right now.

"I don't want to go to bed with you," she said. "I'm not denying that there's a . . . certain . . . something between you and me——"

"You find me as attractive—physically—as I find you." His supremely confident smile created a dazzling contrast between his smooth tanned skin and his sparkling white teeth. "Face it, Nairne. And you know that if you and I were to make love . . ." he had lowered his voice so that it was husky, provocative ". . . that would be something else again. There's a chemistry between us that's explosive."

She wasn't used to open talk of sex . . . but she certainly wouldn't want Strome Galbraith to know it. Wouldn't want him to know it made her uncomfortable . . .

"If we were to make love," she responded in a voice that sounded laughably prim in her own ears, "yes, I suppose it would be . . . what you said——"

"Bliss? Paradise? Ecstasy?" Now there was a teasing undertone to his words.

Nairne felt her cheeks grow very warm, but she lifted her shoulders in as nonchalant a shrug as she could muster. "All three, if you wish." She twisted her lips in a smile that she hoped would convey the disdain she wanted to convey as she added, "And who knows? The earth might even move—we might even generate enough electricity between us to light up the world! But, since it's never going to happen, I can't for the life of me think why we're even discussing it."

"You're afraid of me."

She compressed her lips as she looked down at him. He was leaning back against the cushions with his arms clasped behind his head, in an attitude that implied that he felt totally at home in her living room, and totally in charge of the situation. It was an attitude that for some reason made her see red.

"I'm not afraid of you," she snapped. "And this conversation has become quite ridiculous. If you want

to know the truth, I'm ashamed of the way I acted just
now——"

"You did nothing to be ashamed of."

She knew that the anger she felt wasn't really directed
at him, but at herself, because she had let him kiss her.
No, not because she had let him kiss her, but because
she had cooperated so enthusiastically when he had taken
her in his arms. "That, I think, is for me to decide. I
have to live with myself. And if you and I were to make
love—which heaven forbid!—for me it would be an act
of betrayal."

He looked up at her for a long moment, and then he
said quietly, with no hint of the former teasing in his
tone, "How can you betray a dead man?"

Nairne winced at the baldness of his words, but,
fighting the sudden tightening of her throat muscles, she
managed to say, "Rory's still alive...and always will
be. In my heart."

He didn't respond to her words at first, but there was
a stillness about him that seemed to create an answering
stillness in her. She felt calm, and steady.

"Ah," he said finally. "The heart." He drew in a deep
breath, and smiled, a slow, lazy smile, a smile that moved
his lips but didn't reach his eyes. Eyes that captured hers,
eyes that were mocking. "We started talking about
sex...but you ended up talking about love. Women tend
to do that, don't they?"

There was such cynicism in his voice that Nairne was
reminded of their meeting at the cemetery, when she'd
seen the bleakness, the emptiness in his eyes, and had
wanted to reach out and comfort him. Again she felt
that same sense of wanting to help.

"It's what makes the world go round." Lord, how
trite. Was that all she could come up with? Here was a
man who was suffering, a man who had been hurt, and
all she could say was, "*It's what makes the world go
round*"?

"Oh, no, my dear Nairne, that's where you're wrong.
It's not love that makes the world go round. It's sex that

makes the world go round. Even if no human being ever again fell in love, the world would just keep on going round and round and round. How? Here's the recipe: take one man, and any woman, toss in a smidgen of desire——''

''It's quite obvious you don't have a romantic bone in your body——''

''Romance? You want romance?'' Strome chuckled. ''So mix in lightly one bottle of wine, one soft summer evening, one Julio Iglesias tape... But without these latter ingredients, believe me, the results would be the same. The propagation of the species would be assured. And the world would just keep on turning.''

''Is that what your world is like, Strome?'' Nairne asked quietly. ''Is that the kind of world you want to live in? A world where there's no commitment——?''

''Do you believe in freedom, Nairne?''

''Of course I believe in freedom! But——''

''When you talk about commitment, what you're really talking about is restriction of freedom. Can't two people just enjoy each other, without the need to make all sorts of promises? Look, let me show you what I mean.'' In one swift, fluid movement he got to his feet, and before she could step away he'd taken hold of her hands, one in each of his, and twisted them around his back with the result that she was to all intents and purposes embracing him. ''Now,'' he said softly, ''here we are. One man, one woman, and—I think we both admit—more than a smidgen of desire. Would there be anything wrong in us making love? With no strings?''

Nairne fought to keep a grip on herself. With her arms around him, and his blue eyes smiling so irresistibly down into hers, the male scent of him choking her nostrils, it was hard indeed to come up with some reason as to why they shouldn't——

''Don't you want to take the risk, Nairne? Surrender to the yearnings of your body, to the luxury of enjoying the sensual pleasures of the flesh, with no promises asked, no promises given?'' He pulled her against him more tightly, so she could feel his hard outline against her. "Take a chance," he murmured. "For once in your life, take a chance. Let's finish what we started a few minutes ago. You know you want to. You've more or less admitted that. So...what have you got to lose?"

As she stood there, staring up at him dizzily, she heard Shadow barking. He'd been dozing, she knew, in his warm spot near the Aga, but she recognized his short, sharp bark for what it was—the signal that he needed to go out.

"What do I have to lose?" With a deft little flick of her wrists she extricated herself from his grip, and he didn't try to stop her as she stepped back. "My self-respect," she said, tilting her chin up at him challeng-ingly. "That's what. And now—" she moved toward the door without giving him a further glance "—if you'll excuse me, I have to take Shadow for a walk before I go to bed."

She had to get away from him, to sort out the con-fused emotions in her heart, emotions that were tugging her in a direction she didn't want to go. If he only knew, she reflected unhappily, just how very much she had, during those moments in his arms, wanted to take that chance he'd talked about...

"I'll bid you good-night, then, Mrs. Campbell..."

As she looked around, startled, she found that he was right behind her. So close that she could see the small white flecks in his eyes, the deep lines bracketing his beautiful, mockingly curved mouth. "Good night," she replied tersely, opening the door, glad to get away.

He didn't come after her. But as she crossed the hall, her steps crisp and arrogant and dismissing, she could have sworn he spoke again from his position in the doorway. Only one word. But it was one that arrowed straight into her heart and hit its mark...

"Coward!"

CHAPTER SIX

"DAMN! Damn! Damn!"

Nairne slumped back against the seat of her van for a long moment, hardly aware of the gentle heat of the morning sun against her cheeks as she came to terms with the situation. Then with a sigh of frustration she tugged the key from the ignition and, cramming it back into her pocket, snatched open the door. She had just jumped down onto the gravel and slammed the door shut again—with a vehemence that was quite unnecessary and did nothing to improve her mood—when she saw Strome come out of the house, his tall figure striking in a black leather jacket and dark pants.

"I thought you were going out?" His silky black hair lifted in the breeze, and he swept it back with one hand. "Change of plan? Or did you just forget something?"

"I forgot something all right." Nairne's mouth twisted in a vexed grimace. "I forgot to fill my tank with gas. I don't know how I could have been so careless. And the pumps won't be open for another half hour."

"No problem—I'll drive you wherever you want to go."

Nairne hesitated, shielding her eyes from the sun's rays as she looked at him and weighed her decision. She'd been glad when Dr. Coghill had come by with Annie's key and asked her if she could pack some of Annie's things and take them to the home; it had given her a splendid opportunity to avoid spending time in Strome's company. But now her choice was between wasting half an hour of her very busy morning, and sitting in his car with him for a few minutes...

"Thanks, I really appreciate the offer." Nairne moved to the back of her van and opened the doors.

"Where are we going?" he asked. "Inverness? Elgin? Or," his voice was coaxing, hopeful, "Skye? I've never been to Skye."

Despite herself, Nairne chuckled. "No, we are not going to Skye! We're going to South Street, which is only about half a mile from here, and the only reason I'm taking advantage of your offer is that I have to take these——" she gestured at a pile of folded cardboard boxes in the van "—to Annie's."

He helped her transfer the boxes to the trunk of the Mercedes, before ushering her into the luxurious vehicle. Only after he had pulled away, did he say, in noncommittal tones, "You're doing the packing for Kilty's great-aunt?"

"That's right. Apparently she's very worried about her things, and so Dr. Coghill asked me if I'd mind taking some of her clothes and personal effects to the home, so that they'll be waiting in her room when the ambulance brings her from Raigmore on the weekend."

While Nairne was speaking she caught a hint of the spicy fragrance she had first noticed the night Strome had arrived. Then she had thought the sophisticated fragrance might be that of cologne; now she knew it was not cologne but after-shave. She'd been tidying up his bathroom that morning while he ate breakfast, and when she'd noticed the heavy, squat bottle with the black and white label she'd found herself lifting it up and holding it to her nostrils. She had closed her eyes as the scent seemed to bring his dark, sophisticated presence into the small room beside her, sending a shiver skittering along her skin, disturbing all her sensitive nerve endings. Quickly she had replaced the bottle, but as she left the room she'd caught a glimpse of her reflection in the mirror—eyes guilty, cheeks flushed, lips pinker and fuller than usual...

She started as she realized the man of her thoughts was talking to her.

"Sorry?"

"I merely asked you for directions," he said, obviously amused. "I'm not a mind reader."

Thank heaven!

"And why would we be thanking heaven?" Laughter made his voice light. "Were you thinking thoughts that you didn't want to share?"

Lordy, she had spoken aloud! "Oh, you have to turn here—yes, turn right. South Street—this is where Annie stays. That small house with the shiny brown door, beside the lamppost." Nairne grasped her bag, and as he drew in she fumbled with the door handle. "Thanks," she stepped out onto the pavement, and just before shutting the door she added, "I really appreciate your taking me round here. If you're to be in for lunch today, I'll see you back at the house—around one."

"Aren't you forgetting something?" He had got out of the car too, and was walking around to the trunk.

Damn, the boxes. She had wanted to make a speedy getaway, but it was, apparently, not going to be possible. She waited as he extricated the folded boxes from the boot and carted them across the pavement.

"Thanks again," she said, "I can manage them now." But when she turned to unlock the door she realized that Strome wasn't leaving; he was standing right behind her. She jerked her head up to look at him as he grasped one of her wrists with cool, firm fingers. "No, you don't," he said.

"Don't what?"

"Don't get away that easily," he said, rubbing his thumb along the sensitive inner part of her wrist. "I'm curious to know why you said 'Thank heaven!'"

Oh, he really didn't know when to stop, did he? Well, all right, Nairne said to herself, what the heck...?

"I said 'Thank heaven!' because you said you weren't a mind reader, and I had just been thinking about you. There, does that satisfy you?"

"Oh, my dear Mrs. Campbell, it will take a heck of a lot more than a few *words* to satisfy me!" His grin was so blatantly sexy that Nairne felt a pink blush bloom on her face. "But maybe if you tell me just exactly *what* you had been thinking about me...?"

"If you really want to know," she lied glibly, "I was wondering where you bought that very expensive after-shave you wear."

White teeth gleamed against tanned skin as he grinned down at her. "Oh," he drawled, "the after-shave. City Man, it's called—part of Dominic Wilder's new line. But I didn't buy it. Someone bought it for me."

For "someone," read "some woman'—it was implicit in his tone! Nairne was amazed—and furious with herself—at the way her heart seemed to nosedive as she pictured a sleepy-eyed blonde wearing nothing but a smile, presenting Strome with the intimate gift, probably in the morning after a night of wild and disgustingly uninhibited lovemaking...

Strome was watching her, she saw, and his blue eyes were twinkling with amusement. He had said he wasn't a mind reader, but for one unbalancing moment she found herself wondering if perhaps he was. Oh, how ridiculous...

"Well, aren't you the lucky one?" she said brightly. "Now——" she became aware all at once that he was still holding her wrist "—will you please let me go? I have a lot to do——"

"Good morning, Nairne."

As someone called to her from across the street Nairne twisted her head around so abruptly that she wondered why her neck didn't snap. She thought she had recognized the voice, and as she saw its owner she groaned under her breath. Of all the people she would have wanted *not* to see her in this situation, Fanny Webster would have headed the list. Even at this distance, she could see the curiosity glittering in the retired post-mistress's eyes behind her thick-lensed glasses.

Nairne forced a smile even as she tugged, without success, to free her wrist. "Good morning, Fanny."

Now it would be all over Glencraig before the day was out, that she had been standing on South Street, before nine in the morning, holding hands with the dark stranger who had been in the Royal the other night——

"Worried, Nairne?" Strome's lopsided grin made it clear that he was enjoying her discomfiture.

She looked up at him, her expression taut. "Of course not," she snapped. "Why on earth should I be worried?"

"She's going to be talking about you, isn't she?"

Nairne ignored the tingling sensations shooting up her arm as he rubbed his thumb caressingly under the cuff of her shirt. "So," she said with a nonchalance she was far from feeling, "she's a gossip. If you live in a place like Glencraig you have to expect that everyone is going to know your business, almost before you know it yourself."

He flicked a sideways glance across the street from under his lashes. "She's stopped—ostensibly to look in that café window—but of course she's watching us. Looking at our reflection in the glass. I think she's disappointed, though, that all we're doing is holding hands——"

"We're not holding hands," Nairne hissed. "You are imprisoning my wrist——"

" —and, since I am a generous man, I think we should give her something to talk about."

Nairne's brain seemed to be fuzzy. For the space of five seconds she just stared up into eyes that were gleaming with laughter... laughter and something else. Something that she couldn't define, until he began to lower his head. Then, with the speed of lightning flashing across a stormy sky, she knew what it was. Desire.

"No——"

But he didn't hear her protest; it was obliterated by the lips that captured hers, captured them in a kiss that seemed to go on forever. His mouth was firm, the smooth flesh tasting of peppermint; the skin of his jaw was smooth too, and Nairne's nostrils were tantalized by the spicy, sophisticated fragrance of his City Man. It made sense, she thought distractedly as she fought to stop her body from leaning into him as it seemed so very determined to do, it made sense that someone else would buy after-shave for him; she just couldn't imagine him taking the time to shop for it himself...

He had released her wrist and had slipped his hands inside her open denim jacket, and before she knew it he was caressing her back firmly, possessively. Up and down her spine skimmed his fingertips, following the delicate ridge of bone, pausing for an infinitesimal fraction of a second at the clasp of her bra each time he encountered it through the brushed cotton of her periwinkle shirt. And where were her own hands? To her horror, Nairne realized that she had put them around him, under his black leather jacket, and was clutching his cashmere sweater like a drowning person hanging on to a lifeline.

If only his kiss weren't so sweet, so compellingly sweet. If only he hadn't slipped his tongue past her parted lips, if only he weren't pulling her against him so that she could feel his heartbeats through the fine fabric of her shirt. If only this damned electricity weren't surging between them, heating her blood, making her nipples tingle, draining her of any strength to resist him. If he didn't stop kissing her soon she was going to suffocate and slump over in a dead faint—and boy, would Fanny Webster have a story to tell then!

She knew she should have felt relieved when, finally, the kiss came to an end. But even as she was drawing a deep breath into her lungs, and about to step back, Strome framed her face between his hands. "I have a confession to make," he said huskily, the intense look in his eyes causing an almost painful spiraling sensation to coil through her whole body, finally to settle in some indefinable spot deep inside her. "I didn't kiss you to give Fanny something to talk about." He brushed the pad of his right thumb across her full lower lip, letting the tip of his index finger linger at one corner. "I kissed you because I couldn't help myself. You are just so damned beautiful."

Why did he keep saying she was beautiful? Nairne wondered despairingly. Why make things more complicated? Why couldn't he just tell the truth—he was a red-blooded male and he was lusting after her purely because of this confounded chemistry thing between them. Just as she, shamefully, was lusting after him! And if he didn't take the tip of his finger from the corner of her mouth, if he didn't right this very minute stop teasing her inner flesh in that tantalizingly seductive way, the last vestiges of her resolution were going to melt away and she would brush her lips across that long, hard finger—maybe even draw the tip into her mouth!—and she knew only too well where that would lead—regardless of whether or not Fanny Webster was watching the whole show reflected in the window of the King's Café!

And never before, in all her twenty-nine years, had she been guilty of such wantonly erotic thoughts. Was she going *mad*?

With a little moan of desperation she wrenched herself aside, and, slipping past Strome, tried to regulate her breathing so that it sounded more normal. "I really must go now," she said in a rush, unlocking Annie's shiny brown door and pushing it open. "I do have a lot to——"

She broke off with a gasp of denial as he followed her inside and shut the door behind them.

"I'll help you," he said.

"No." Oh, Lord, where had that mouse squeak come from? "No!" she repeated in a voice that was almost a shout. And "No," a third time, and she was relieved to hear that her voice once more sounded as if it belonged to her. "Thank you, but I know Annie Low, and I know it would upset her if she found out that some stranger—especially a man—was handling her private things."

Nairne switched on the hall light; how was she going to
get rid of him? She had the feeling that if he stayed, and
they were together for any length of time in the confines
of this tiny house, they would eventually bump into each
other, and as soon as their bodies touched she'd be in
his arms again. And that, she intended to avoid at all
costs.

She turned to face him and found that he was standing
right behind her, his hands jammed casually into his
pockets. Despite her own above-average height, he
towered over her. She took a step back. "If you really
want to help," she said quickly, "how about coming back
around twelve? I should be finished by then, and you
can lift the heavier boxes into your trunk and we can
take them to the home before lunch. Then, on the way
back to Bruach, we can stop for a can of gas——"

All of a sudden, Nairne noticed that Strome was no
longer listening to her. He was staring past her shoulder,
through the open doorway into a small room behind her.
She turned to follow his glance. It was Kilty's room, a
small space with a large window, whose light played on
the wall across from it. And it was that wall Strome was
looking at, with a strange expression on his face, the
wall on which Kilty had his display of photographs.

He seemed totally unaware of Nairne's presence, and
it was plain that he'd completely banished from his mind
the kiss they had just shared out on the pavement. He
sidestepped her and moved into the room, taking his
hands out of his pockets as he did so, his bearing no
longer casual, his attention concentrated. "My God,"
he said, an edge of surprise in his voice, "who did
these?"

"This is Kilty's room."

"Yes, yes," he said, shaking his head as if to dismiss
her words. "Kilty's room. But who took these
photographs?"

"Kilty did. Aren't they wonderful?"

For the longest time he didn't respond; he just stared at the photographs. Outside in the street Nairne could hear a dog barking, could hear the sound of the school bus stopping outside the King's Café, could hear children's laughter as light footsteps ran past the front door.

She cleared her throat. "You do...think they're good, don't you?"

At last he finished examining the photographs and turned to face her. "Mm?" He raked a hand through his dark hair, tousling it so that it fell over his forehead. "What did you say?"

"He has such a gift, hasn't he?" She said it quietly, and it wasn't a question, but a statement. Looking at a blowup of an eagle rising from the topmost branches of a huge spruce tree, she went on, "I'm so disappointed he's given it up."

"*He's given it up?*"

"Yes, just lately." She shrugged. "He told me it was because there wasn't enough space here for him to have a darkroom, but I think there was more to it than that— though I don't know what it could be. The worst part is, he sold his Nikon. It was a beauty—Hugh gave it to him three Christmases ago. He could ill afford it, but Hughie Dunbar would have cut his heart out for that boy. Kilty was in seventh heaven..."

Strome turned abruptly away from her and walked stiffly to the window. With his back to the room he stood there for so long that Nairne began to wonder if there was something wrong with him. Should she go over to him, touch his arm, ask if she could help? She shook her head. Something told her, some deep instinct, that Strome didn't want to be approached. He was obviously in some other world, lost in thoughts that were strictly, intensely private. Thoughts he wouldn't want to share with her. These thoughts had something to do with Kilty, of that she was sure. And she was just as sure that he wanted to be alone.

It was a great puzzle, she reflected as she tiptoed from the room. And a puzzle to which only Strome and Kilty seemed to possess the parts...or at least, some of the parts. She closed the door quietly behind her, her thoughts awhirl as she walked along the hall to Annie's room.

What on earth was going on? she wondered. Everything seemed to have become so complicated since Strome Galbraith had arrived in Glencraig.

The sooner he was gone, the better. Then she'd be able to settle down to her peaceful life again...

A life that was going to be richer, and more joyful, now that Kilty was going to be part of it.

But, as she opened the first drawer and started sorting Annie's clothes, she realized to her dismay that the prospect of saying goodbye to Strome Galbraith and never seeing him again didn't bring with it the feeling of thankfulness that she had expected.

And when, a few moments later as she was folding one of Annie's Shetland-knit cardigans, she heard him go out and heard the front door slam behind him she held the sweater against her chest with tightly clutching fingers and stared unseeingly into space for the longest time.

"There!" Nairne closed the lid of the last cardboard box and stood back, hands on hips, looking around Annie's bedroom. It looked so bare now, with all the knickknacks packed away. All the drawers were empty, and she had had just enough boxes to do the job.

A loud knock at the front door made her start and glance at her watch. It was just quarter to twelve, but perhaps Strome had come back early.

She felt her pulse quicken as she walked along the hall. What sort of a mood would he be in now? she wondered. Would he still be distracted, tense, the way he'd been when he'd looked at Kilty's display of photographs on the wall?

She forced a smile as she opened the door, but when she saw that it wasn't Strome on the pavement outside, but Flora MacDonald, the minister's wife, she felt herself relax.

"Flora, how nice to see you!" She greeted the small gray-haired woman with a smile that was no longer forced but genuinely welcoming. "I'm afraid if you've come to see Annie, though, she's not here——"

"Oh, no, dear, I've not come to see Annie. I know she's in Raigmore. No, I bumped into Fanny earlier and she said she'd seen you here..."

And what else had she said? Nairne wondered wryly.

"It...it's you I want to talk with. I'd been intending going to Bruach to talk with you this evening but I thought I'd chance popping along by Annie's just now in case you were still here." She bit her lip and looked down at the small bag she was carrying.

As she looked up again Nairne noticed that the older woman's eyes were clouded with worry. What could be wrong? she wondered. "Won't you come in?" Nairne stepped back and gestured toward the small entryway.

"I don't have time, Nairne, I have to get home and make sandwiches for the guild meeting this afternoon."

"Oh, the meeting. I'd almost forgotten about it..."

Nairne heard the smooth hum of a car coming along the street, and from the corner of her eye she saw Strome's Mercedes pull in at the curb a few yards away.

Really, there was something about his timing, she decided impatiently, that left a lot to be desired. She touched Flora's arm gently. "What can I do for you, Flora?"

The minister's wife tightened her grip on the plastic bag. "I hate to bother you, but Dr. Coghill mentioned to Peter that Kilty's staying with you at Bruach just now, that you're looking after him, so I thought you'd be the person I should see——"

"Kilty?" Nairne frowned, trying to ignore the way her heart lurched as Strome shut the door of his car and started walking across toward them.

"Kilty sold his camera to Duncan." Flora's voice softened as she talked about her only child, a clever lad of seventeen who was going away to university the following year. "He took money out of his bank account to pay for it," Flora's lower lip trembled, "money that had been set aside for his education. We had a long talk last night, Peter, Duncan, and I, and Duncan finally admitted it had been a whim on his part. He's changed his mind—he doesn't want Kilty's camera." She took in a deep breath, and when she went on her eyes were pleading. "Nairne, can you talk to Kilty, try to get Duncan's money back? He really needs it."

Strome had come to a halt close by, and Nairne had no doubt that he'd heard most of the conversation. But she was too concerned with Flora's distress to let his presence bother her. "Kilty didn't want to sell the camera, I'm sure of that. But Flora, dear, I have no idea what he did with the money. He might have needed it for something."

She bit her lip as she saw tears well up in the older woman's eyes. "Oh, dear, I never thought of that, never thought he might have already spent it."

"The camera's there, in that bag?"

Nairne blinked as Strome's voice abruptly broke in between herself and Flora.

"Oh, Flora," she offered stiffly after a brief pause, "this is Strome Galbraith. He's staying at Bruach...a B and B. Strome, this is Mrs. MacDonald—Flora's husband, Peter, is the minister at the parish kirk."

Flora shook hands with Strome, and then, obviously surrendering to the authority implicit in his words and bearing, though she had never met him before, she opened the plastic bag and held it out to him. "This camera—my son Duncan bought it from——"

"Yes, I heard." Strome's voice was reassuring. "And I sympathize with you in your predicament. Let me see the camera."

Flora took the Nikon from the bag, and Strome handled the expensive piece of equipment carefully as he gave it a thorough examination.

"How much did your boy pay for it?" he asked quietly.

Flora murmured the answer to his question in such a soft voice that Nairne could barely hear it, but hear it she did, and she almost exclaimed aloud. Hazel had told her that Hugh had paid a lot for the camera, but she hadn't realized just how valuable it was. She watched, feeling dizzy, as Strome put the camera back in the bag, and when he asked her, "Would you mind holding this?" she accepted it wordlessly.

In one smooth movement he drew a checkbook from the inside pocket of his leather jacket, and in a matter of seconds had written out a check. Folding it neatly, he slipped it into Flora's hand. "There," he said, giving her a warm smile. "Now put that in your son's bank account, and tell him not to be so quick off the mark next time he sees something he *thinks* he wants. I'll settle matters with Kilty."

A moment later, eyes glistening with relief, Flora was bustling away along the street... and Nairne was left standing outside Annie's shiny brown door with Strome, feeling as if someone had taken her emotions and given them a good shake which had left them swirling around in confusion. And because of that confusion... and because of the traitorous way her senses were reacting to Strome as he stood there, tall and bone-meltingly attractive, with the breeze gusting his hair over his brow and his intense sapphire eyes reflecting the blue of the sky above, she said, much more angrily than she felt, "Don't you think what you did there was just a wee bit presumptuous? I'm not taking away from the generosity of your actions—you've taken a huge load off Flora's

shoulders, she was obviously worried sick about the
money—but really, this whole thing was none of your
business! And that was certainly not the way to handle
it!''

He looked down at Nairne, the slight twitching of a
muscle in his jaw the only sign that he wasn't quite as
calm as he would have had her believe. ''No, it wasn't
the right way to handle it. But it was expedient. And
you don't have any need to worry. As I said, I'll settle
matters with Kilty.''

''You mean, you'll ask him to recompense you for the
money you just gave Flora.''

''Right.''

''And what if he doesn't have it? What then?''

''I'm aware he might already have spent some, or all
of the money.'' His lips tightened. ''We'll work something out.''

Nairne grabbed a handful of tousled auburn curls the
wind was blowing around her cheeks and held them back
from her face as she glared up at him. ''Have you forgotten what I said about Kilty having given up photography? He may not want the Nikon——''

''The boy has talent,'' Strome snapped. ''When God
gives a talent such as his you don't just 'give it up.' You
have a responsibility to use it to the full.''

A frustrated exclamation burst from between Nairne's
lips. *I agree*, she wanted to cry, *I do agree*. But Strome
hadn't seen how distraught Kilty had been when he'd
told her he was no longer interested in photography; she
had. How was the lad going to react when Strome presented him with the Nikon and demanded payment?

The church clock struck the hour, and she drew in a
shivering sigh. There was no point in standing out here
in the street arguing with this man; it would get her
nowhere.

''Come on in,'' she said wearily. ''I have all the boxes
ready. Thanks so much for coming back.''

"No problem. Now, what time does Kilty get out of school?"

"Four o'clock."

"On the way to the home, show me where his school is. I'll meet him at four, and we'll have a talk."

Nairne shook her head. "Not today, I'm afraid. He's gone on a class outing to Aberdeen—to a showing of *Hamlet* at the theater. They won't be back till quite late tonight. And he'll be tired. Best leave it till tomorrow." It was strange; she had sensed such tension in Strome when he looked at Kilty—and if her assumption was correct, the assumption that Strome had known and hated Hazel, the tension must be linked to that...yet he had done this thing, bought the camera back, because he saw Kilty had talent.

Was there more to it? More than she could see? Questions concerning the two bombarded her mind—questions that at the moment, with the limited knowledge she had, were unanswerable——

"Tomorrow it is, then." Strome's voice interrupted her thoughts. "And today, after we deliver these boxes, I'll take you out for a bar lunch."

No, thought Nairne, that wouldn't be a good idea. Better to spend as little time with this man as possible. He was having a very unsettling effect on her. "Oh, that's kind of you," she was glad she had an excuse to beg off, "but I'm afraid I'm committed to going to a guild meeting this afternoon."

"Dinner, then. Unless," his eyes mocked hers as if he could read her thoughts, "you've already made plans for the evening too?"

She never could tell a lie. "No...no, I haven't made any plans for the evening."

"Then I'll phone and book a table at the Heatherview."

"Oh, but..." Nairne bit her lip. She and Rory had always gone to the Heatherview for dinner when they had something special to celebrate—and they had always sat at one of Hazel's tables. She had been a waitress there ever since Kilty had started school. Nairne hadn't been in the place for over a year, knowing that a visit would only bring back memories, memories that would be very upsetting.

"Settled, then? The Heatherview?"

Nairne sighed. Why not? she asked herself. She couldn't avoid going to the Heatherview for the rest of her life; there had to be a first time to go back, and it might as well be tonight.

Her lips curved in a smile that felt stiff. "Settled, then. The Heatherview."

CHAPTER SEVEN

THE night was dark, and as Strome and Nairne left the Mercedes and crossed the crowded parking lot on arrival at the Heatherview a mist swirled in from the moor and swathed them in its cold gray cloak. Nairne grimaced, knowing that the fine droplets would be transforming her hair into a mass of ridiculously frizzy curls.

In the foyer Strome slid off her coat and, as he did, his gaze skimmed over her gold silk blouse and her flared skirt with its muted gold and terracotta check, and there was no mistaking his approval.

"Beautiful," he murmured, caressing her arm briefly with his fingertips. His touch sent a little shiver through Nairne, a shiver that intensified as his gaze lingered on her hair. The frizzy curls obviously didn't look ridiculous to him. There was no mistaking the admiration in his eyes. She felt her cheeks turn warm.

"You look," he said softly, "as if you've just stepped out of one of Rembrandt's later paintings, all golden and mellow and utterly enchanting."

His compliment heightened her color till she was sure her cheeks must be a psychedelic red that Rembrandt in his wildest dreams couldn't have imagined. To hide her embarrassment, she said in a flippant tone, "My, you city men do have a way with words!"

She thought she heard him chuckle as he gave her coat to the cloakroom attendant. "Why is it," he cupped her elbow and began leading her across the carpeted foyer, "that you find it so difficult to accept a compliment gracefully?"

Why is it, she wondered dizzily, that I find it so difficult to think when you're touching me? "Many women are guilty of that," she said. "Probably because when we're little girls our mothers teach us not to be vain."

"And men? As little boys, are they also taught not to be vain?"

"I've no idea—I don't know how little boys are brought up, as I don't have any brothers. Surely you know the answer to that? How about yourself? Did *your* mother teach you not to be vain? Or perhaps you were never a little boy!"

They had reached the entrance to the dining room, and as they paused in the doorway Nairne looked up questioningly at Strome. To her surprise, she saw what she thought was a spasm of pain across his features, but before it had really registered with her it had gone...and his lips had curved in a smile. Must have been a trick of the light, Nairne decided...

"Perhaps you're right," he said easily. "Perhaps I never was a little boy."

"In that case," she retorted, "you probably have no problem accepting compliments!"

"Why don't you try me?"

"Try you?"

"Pay me a compliment, Mrs. Campbell...see how I react."

"Oh...I...don't think..."

One dark brow quirked mockingly. "Nothing about me that you like? Surely I can't be so impossibly unattractive that——"

"Unattractive? Oh, you're not unattractive——" Damn, Nairne thought, I fell right into that one!

"Sorry, compliments couched in negative terms don't count. Give it another shot."

She was being foolish...by being so reluctant to go along with his little game, she was going to make him curious as to her reasons, and she didn't want that. But what could she say that wouldn't be too personal? How about "You have very nice eyes"? Yes, that would do, because they really were very nice.

She cleared her throat. ''Your eyes...it's strange, but when you look down at me like that it's almost as if you're hypnotizing me...'' She swayed. Surely she hadn't said that...she hadn't meant to say——

''Very good.'' Those incredibly blue eyes danced into hers. ''That's the most intriguing compliment I've had in years—I'll certainly take advantage of the inside information when the right moment presents itself! Thank you, Mrs. Campbell. Notice how I did that, by the way— just a simple 'Thank you'? Do you think you could bring yourself to do the same——?''

''Nairne, *ma chère!*'' The headwaiter materialized in front of them, dapper in his black suit. He didn't appear to notice Strome; all his attention was focused on Nairne. ''*Quel plaisir* to see you again! And looking so *ravissant*! You will light up my dining room—everyone will be blinded by your beauty!''

It was on the tip of Nairne's tongue to say, as she'd always done before in the face of the waiter's gushing compliments, ''Oh, Alain, you're such a flatterer,'' when she felt Strome dig her in the ribs. She wriggled impatiently from his touch, but did change her intended response to a smiling, ''Why, Alain, thank you.''

She knew Strome's murmured, ''Bravo!'' was meant for her ears alone.

''*Ma chère,*'' Alain's voice had become soft, sympathetic, ''I am so sorry to learn about your 'usband. And this is why you 'ave stayed away from this place? The 'appy memories, they are painful?''

''Yes.'' Nairne's tone was a little husky. ''The memories are painful...''

''Ah...but as time goes by they will become less so. This I promise you. And now...?'' For the first time the headwaiter transferred his gaze to Strome, and gave a start of recognition. ''Monsieur Galbraith, welcome back to our establishment.''

There was no mistaking the deference in his manner, and Nairne deduced that the tip Strome had slipped to the headwaiter on his previous visit must have been a memorable one.

With an extravagant flourish of his enormous leather-covered menus Alain announced, "Follow me. You will 'ave the best table in the dining room."

After seating them, he draped Nairne's crisp linen napkin over her lap and she looked up at him with a smile. "The dining room's busy, as always, I see."

"*Oui*, always busy. And 'ow I miss the dark one—she cannot be replaced. Such a worker." He rolled his liquid brown eyes upward. "A saint, that one. A saint."

Shaking his head sadly, he went on, "And now I will send the wine waiter to you," before giving a small bow and taking his leave.

From Nairne's seat she could see the huge brick fireplace, with its sparking logs and tongues of bright flame leaping up the chimney. How many times she had sat with Rory, she thought, looking at that same——

"Seeing pictures in the fire?"

Startled, she turned her attention to Strome. "Sorry," she said. "I was just..."

"Looking into the past? From what Alain said, I gather you and your husband used to dine here...and this is your first visit since...his death?"

"Mm. I'm afraid I've been avoiding it——"

"Why didn't you say something when I suggested we dine here——? Oh, but you did hesitate. I should have realized——"

"Of course you shouldn't—how could you?" Nairne found herself wanting to dispel the frown of apology clouding his eyes. "And I'm glad we came." She made a determined effort to lighten the atmosphere. "I'm here...and the first time is always the worst. I feel as if I've achieved a little goal tonight."

"Then," Strome smiled as the wine waiter approached, "we must celebrate. Nothing less than a bottle of Dom Perignon will do..."

And Dom Perignon it was, along with a wonderful dinner. Nairne and Strome both chose the piping hot cock-a-leekie soup, followed by barbecued salmon, and the featherlight raspberry cheesecake recommended by their waitress. Nairne was surprised that not once during their lazy, relaxed meal did conversation lag between herself and Strome—though she didn't realize till she was sipping the last mouthful of her Irish coffee that Strome, skillfully, had encouraged her to do most of the talking. He'd seemed so interested in her, in her work, and in Glencraig in general. He'd laughed aloud several times as she'd told him about some of the local worthies, regaling him with tales of their more eccentric activities.

But not once had he directed the conversation anywhere near Kilty. Nor, thought Nairne, near Hazel...

"And ze dark one?" He sat back in his chair, tilting the legs, and his eyes were filled with amusement. "Ze saint?" White teeth flashed in contrast to tanned skin as his smile broadened. "Who was she, zees saint who 'ad ze *audacité* to quit her job and leave ze *maître d'* in ze *grand* lurch?"

It was as if some unseen being had read her thoughts and transferred them to Strome. Nairne placed her coffee cup carefully into its saucer. "Alain was talking about Hazel," she said in a subdued voice, "Kilty's mother. And you're wrong. Hazel didn't quit, she——" *She died.* As the words echoed in her head Nairne felt a sob clutching her throat and found she couldn't go on. Tears sprang to her eyes with such alacrity that it was as if they were actors who had been standing in the wings, knowing they would be called on and waiting impatiently for their cue. She fumbled in her bag for a Kleenex, and then dabbed clumsily at the welling tears, inwardly cursing her lack of self-control. She had realized that this evening could be an emotional one; she should have been prepared, should have steeled herself.

"Are you all right?"

Strome's concerned voice broke into her thoughts. Swallowing the huge lump in her throat, she shook her head and stuffed the damp Kleenex back into her bag. "Yes," her voice was a little unsteady, "I'm fine now. Sorry. It just got to me for a moment—talking of Hazel."

"You were close?"

"Yes." Nairne managed a watery smile. "Very close."

"She . . . confided in you?"

"Confided in me?"

"You know—told you all the deep, dark secrets in her life."

His tone was strangely challenging. What on earth was he hinting at? "Deep, dark secrets? Hazel Dunbar wasn't the type to have deep, dark secrets. She was——"

"A saint?" He uttered a grim, disparaging laugh. "A 'saintly woman' is an oxymoron, Nairne—the words contradict each other! A saint is, by definition, a very virtuous person, and there isn't a woman alive who qualifies for that distinction. The female sex can't be trusted . . . *that* is a fact of life. The Bard said it all and said it best with his 'Frailty, thy name is——' "

Nairne pushed back her chair roughly and got to her feet. Clasping her bag with both hands, she looked down at Strome. "I won't call you a chauvinistic pig," she said coldly, "because, besides bringing me up not to be vain, my mother brought me up not to call people names, no matter how deserved those names might be. What I will say, however, is this—you have just ruined what was up till a few moments ago the most pleasant evening I've had in months. And now," she swept a hard, scathing glance over him, "I'd like to go home."

Without waiting to see if he was following, she threaded her way swiftly among the tables, and, once in the vestibule, crossed with quick, angry strides to the coat-check counter. While waiting for her coat she muttered furiously under her breath, "Rude, arrogant, overbearing——"

"All three, I'm afraid."

Nairne felt herself being swung around. Strome's grip on her shoulders was so firm that she knew she needn't try to release herself.

"Guilty, ma'am." A swath of dark hair had fallen over his brow, adding irresistible appeal to his features, which were twisted in an apologetic grimace. "Forgive?"

It was on the tip of her tongue to snap, "No! What woman likes to be lumped in with all those who can't be trusted?" but she bit back the words. She knew he hadn't directed his barb at her personally, and she could only guess at the hurts life had dealt him to have caused such a negative attitude toward the opposite sex.

The attendant returned with her coat, and as Strome helped her with it she said, rather wearily, "I'll forgive you for spoiling our evening, but what you said about women...it's not for me to forgive or not to forgive. You've obviously had some bad experiences, which have colored your judgment. Maybe some day you'll meet a woman who is all that you expect a woman to be. I can only hope you'll live up to her expectations of what a man should be."

"Ouch!" He smiled down at her as she turned up the collar of her coat. "That was a low blow."

"But well deserved," Nairne said firmly.

"Granted." When she'd turned up the collar of her coat her long hair had been captured inside; now his warm fingertips brushed her neck as he scooped out the bouncy auburn curls and let them tumble over her shoulders and back. "So..." he subjected her to the full force of his irresistible smile, a smile that sent a honeyed warmth streaming through her body "...friends again?"

The coat-check attendant, a local girl, was watching, listening avidly, and Nairne knew that the little scene would be all over Glencraig by noon the next day. She walked away from the desk before saying archly to Strome, "We were friends before?" She raised her brows in mock surprise.

He walked alongside her, and clasped one of her hands in his as they stepped down the outside steps together.

"Yes," his grip tightened for a moment, "yes, Nairne. We were friends before. In fact, strange as it may seem, and I don't pretend to understand it myself, I feel as if we'll be friends always."

He led her toward the Mercedes, obviously not expecting a response. But, as Nairne once again felt the mist settle on her hair and dampen her cheeks, she realized that she had responded to his words. Not with words of her own, but in the way her pulse had quickened. No, she could never just be a friend to this man; her feelings for him were far too jumbled for that. And far, far too jumbled for her to even begin to sort out.

And she didn't want to sort them out. Deep down she sensed that, if she let him, this man would play havoc with her life, with the serenity and peace of mind she had been struggling to recover ever since Rory's death. She was proud of the distance she'd come in the last year, but she knew she had some way to go yet. Fate had pummeled her heart, and her heart was still bruised. She wasn't about to toss it in the ring again and let fate have another go at it. The only sensible thing to do would be to stay in her corner.

As soon as she and Strome got back to Bruach she would make some excuse and go up to bed. He hadn't said anything about how long he was planning to stay on in Glencraig, but tomorrow she would ask him. She hoped he would leave soon.

She'd wait, though, until he'd had his talk with Kilty, about the camera.

Strome didn't bring the matter up next morning till after breakfast.

They had all three eaten together, and Nairne was rinsing the coffeepot in the sink, and Kilty had just got up from the table, saying, "I'll be off to school, then," when Strome took up a stance with his back to the window, hands jammed into the pockets of his black pants, and said,

"Hang on a minute—I'd like a word with you."

Kilty turned to face him. "I don't have much time," he said, politely enough. "What is it?"

Strome frowned. "Duncan MacDonald's mother came looking for Nairne yesterday, to tell her Duncan bought your camera with money earmarked for his education..."

Nairne saw Kilty's eyelids flicker, but it was the only sign that Strome had elicited any reaction from him, other than an almost imperceptible straightening of his wide shoulders under the thin cotton T-shirt. When he didn't speak, Strome went on,

"Mrs. MacDonald wanted the money back——"

"Dunc and I made a deal." Kilty's face seemed whiter than before, and Nairne thought she detected a hint of panic in his voice as he went on, "I canna give him back the money. He'll have to... keep the camera."

Strome said, "I have the camera."

Shock flickered in Kilty's gray eyes, but he immediately shuttered them, and lifted his shoulders in a shrug. "So——" his voice was just a little unsteady "—keep it. I don't care."

"Dammit," Strome burst out irritably, "I don't want to keep it. I want you to have it. I've seen your photographs—the work you've done. *It's damned good.* You've a lot to learn, of course, but the talent's there. I've paid for the camera, and we'll work something out— you can pay me back in installments. I don't care how long it takes." He took a deep breath, as if trying to control his impatience, and then went on more evenly, "You can't have spent *all* the money. How much do you have left?"

Color tinged Kilty's cheekbones. "None."

"It's all gone?" Incredulity sharpened Strome's tone. "What the *devil* did you spend it on?" He shook his head, his frustration quite evident.

As Nairne watched, somehow, for an infinitesimal fraction of a second, the tableau before her froze in time. The man and the boy were almost identical, she realized—as if made from the same mold. The same tilt of the head, the same planes of the face, the same angle of the jaw. The same strong neck, the same wide shoulders, the same long, capable fingers clenched into the same hard fists——

And then time moved on. She realized that Strome was still talking, and hurriedly, as if in a panic, she pushed into the deepest recesses of her mind the thought that had tried to rise from her subconscious, the thought that was so unthinkable that she just couldn't let it surface...

"What kind of a boy are you," Strome was saying, "who could dispose so casually of an article you should have treasured? According to Nairne, your father made a great sacrifice in order that you could have that camera. What could you possibly have wanted...?"

Kilty swallowed, cleared his throat, rubbed his palms down the side of his kilt. "It wasn't so much something I...wanted," he began hesitantly, "that I spent the money on...it was something I...*needed*...."

There was such an aching uncertainty in his tone, as if he was apprehensive about Strome's response to what he was going to say, that Nairne felt an answering ache in her heart. She wanted to say some words of reassurance, but before she could Strome burst out harshly, "Something you *needed*? Good Lord, you're not on *drugs*, are you?"

Kilty's eyes widened, and he stared at Strome for a moment as if he hadn't understood the words he'd heard. And then, with such anguish on his face that it was as if Strome had actually struck him, he cried in a strangled voice, "No, of course I'm not—no way, man! How could you think——?"

Brushing his forearm across his eyes, he wheeled away, his kilt flying around his knees, and made for the door. As he passed Nairne she saw the clenched misery in his face. But before she could move he had gone, the kitchen door shut behind him.

She turned to Strome, reproachful words on his lips, but the words died away, unsaid, when she saw his ashen color. He stood there, looking as if the life had drained from him, staring blindly at the closed door. Then, with a bitterly despairing "Damn!" he crashed a fist against the wall beside him, with such force that the telephone on Nairne's desk made a trembling tinkle of protest.

"I made a mess of that, didn't I?" The contempt in his tone, contempt for himself, grated on Nairne's ears. "I'd best catch him and make amends before he goes out——"

Nairne caught hold of his arm as he made to pass her. "No," she said, shaking her head. "He'll not thank you for going after him, not the way he's feeling right now. You've hurt him... and hurt him badly. He's a straight kid, always has been. Wait till tonight—he'll have thought things over and realized that your conclusion wasn't all that surprising in view of the circumstances."

"You're probably right." He raked an angry hand through his hair. "But if not...drugs...what in heaven's *name* could he have needed all that money for?"

Nairne looked at him, and saw the utter perplexity in his eyes, but she also saw something else. Something she couldn't decipher. And all of a sudden she felt she'd had enough. She couldn't go on like this any longer, watching the interplay between those two, without trying to find out the reason for the undercurrents swirling between them. After all, this was her home; Kilty was at the moment her protégé...she was involved, like it or not.

She clasped her hands round her upper arms and took in a deep breath. "Strome...normally I don't poke my nose into other people's business, but I wish you'd tell me why you're here. I can't help wondering what the connection is between you and Kilty. You seem to find it difficult to relate to the boy...maybe you even dislike him, yet you——"

She broke off as Strome turned from her and moved to the window. Bracing his hands on the countertop, he stared out into the dark morning, his shoulders rigid. Cutting her off, shutting her off, the way he had done once before, in Kilty's bedroom at Annie's. Then she had walked away. This time she was going to wait. Forever, if necessary.

He must have sensed the stubbornness emanating from her, for, after a time that seemed endless to Nairne, he finally turned back to her. His face was haggard. "You're wrong." His voice was thick with choked-back emotion. "I don't dislike the boy..."

"But there's something...isn't there? That day we met, at the cemetery, you were looking at Hazel's gravestone. I asked you if you'd known her——"

"And I said I was interested in old graveyards."

"Mm. You didn't lie...but you didn't really answer my question, did you?"

"No," he said, his voice rasping. "No, I didn't."

"If I ask you again, will you? Tell me the truth, I mean?"

He closed his eyes for a long moment, and when he opened them again he fixed them on her steadily. "Yes," he said. "I'll tell you the truth this time if you ask again."

Nairne stared up into the depthless blue of his gaze. "Did you know Hazel Dunbar?" she asked softly.

And felt herself frown as he answered, just as softly, "No, I didn't know Hazel Dunbar."

She could have sworn he was telling the truth, but somehow she felt there should have been more to it. She was aware of a sinking sensation of disappointment. There was a puzzle here, and she had thought she was close to finding out the solution. Obviously, she had been wrong.

Strome's eyes, she suddenly noticed, had become bleak. She felt her heart shiver. There *was* more to it; she had been right. And now, she sensed, at last he was going to tell her. She pressed the tips of her fingers against her lips, and waited, barely breathing, for him to speak.

"I didn't know Hazel Dunbar," he repeated in a voice that she hardly recognized, "because I knew her before she was married. Her name at the time was Hazel Lindsay——"

"Yes, she was Hazel Lindsay... But why on earth didn't you tell me you knew her that day at the cemetery—why make such a secret of it?" Nairne shook her head bewilderedly. "I don't understand..."

"No, how could you? It was a secret I wanted to keep. A secret I intended to keep. Since you're planning to adopt Kilty, I'll reveal it to you, but you must swear it will go no further."

"I swear." Nairne's voice was faint. "But——"

"Hazel Lindsay and I were lovers before she married." He ignored Nairne's incredulous gasp. In a voice that was absolutely devoid of emotion he went on, "Somerled Dunbar is my son."

Somerled Dunbar is my son.

For the rest of the morning, as she threw herself into her housecleaning, Nairne found that Strome's words echoed over and over in her head, as if there were a stereo player hidden somewhere in the house with the record stuck, and no matter how much she wanted to she couldn't get the words to stop. By noon her head ached so badly that she knew she had to get out, take a walk, do something to take the pressure off.

The day was clear, with a feel of snow in the air, and, though the sun was bright, it hugged its wintry warmth to itself. Zipping up her quilted green anorak, Nairne

closed the front door behind her, and after whistling for
Shadow she walked down the drive to the main road.

On any other day she'd have walked slowly, enjoying
the beauty of the countryside, but not today. Today there
was room for nothing in her shell-shocked brain but
Strome Galbraith's devastating declaration. She walked
hurriedly, as if by doing so she could escape from her
thoughts. The sound of her boots on the paved road
rang out across the fields, but she was barely aware of
the Aberdeen Angus cattle grazing there, or their solemn
eyes lifted curiously to watch her as she passed.

Strome Galbraith. He had gone out in his Mercedes,
but he was with her as she walked nevertheless. She could
feel his presence so strongly that she wouldn't have been
at all surprised if, on turning quickly, she had found him
walking at her side.

A gust of wind swooped down the road, lifting her
hair and whirling it around her cheeks as she clambered
over the wooden stile that led to the path around the
loch. Once she reached the water's edge Shadow raced
away ahead of her, and she was alone with her thoughts.

And her regrets.

Why, she agonized, had she not tried to stop Strome
when he'd wheeled away after his shattering an-
nouncement? He'd thrown out over his shoulder that he
was going for a drive and would be back after lunch,
and moments later she'd heard him close the front door.
Every instinct had urged her to run after him, call him
back, plead with him to tell her more, give some
explanation...

Because she desperately needed an explanation. Hazel
Dunbar had been a longtime friend. She thought she'd
known Hazel, and known her well. Yet for fourteen
years—if Strome was telling the truth—the lovely dark-
eyed woman had been living a lie.

Hugh had not been Kilty's father.

Now Kilty's real father had turned up...

But why now? Why hadn't he supported Hazel in her pregnancy? Why hadn't he married her? Why...?

Nairne uttered a frustrated exclamation. So many questions. But the past was past. Strome had turned up... and the only possible reason for that was... he wanted the boy.

She, too, wanted the boy; wanted to adopt him. And there had been no doubt in her mind the other night that Kilty had been happy with the idea. But he didn't know that this man—this stranger—was his father. When he discovered that, what would he want to do?

Distractedly Nairne pushed aside a thorny branch that was in her way. She had an ominous feeling that, whatever was decided, someone was going to get hurt.

She winced as she felt pain stabbing again at her temples, and she realized that her headache, instead of disappearing, had only become worse. She'd have been wiser, she realized, to have taken a couple of aspirin and gone to bed for an hour.

Maybe that was what she should still do.

She halted for a moment under a huge, lichen-encrusted fir tree. "Shadow," she called.

And, as the collie came loping back along the path, Nairne shivered and jammed her hands farther into her pockets. "Come on, boy," she murmured, "let's go home."

The mailman was cycling down the main road toward her as she reached the gates of Bruach.

"It's a lovely day, Callum." She managed to conjure up a smile as he drew near.

"Aye, Nairne, a grand day—though there's a new fall of snow up on the hills. Slagmhor got the brunt of it, I'm thinking—but the weatherman predicts good weather for the next few days." He slowed for a moment as he came alongside her. "No mail for you today—no news is good news, I always say!" With a chuckle and a tip of his peaked hat he was off again, whistling the latest hit song as he went.

As Nairne walked briskly along the drive she glanced up at Slagmhor, the mountain's peaked shape rising up beyond the solid turreted outlines of Bruach. Yes, Callum was right—there had certainly been snow overnight on the hills, and Slagmhor looked as beautiful as she'd ever seen it, the snow-covered peak jutting picturesquely against the sky.

Looking at it, she realized, was calming, its serenity somehow soothing her troubled thoughts. And she noticed, as she opened the front door, that her headache had gone; her walk, after all, had done her good. Humming softly, she shrugged off her jacket and tossed it over the newel post. A cup of tea, she decided, was what she needed.

But she was only halfway to the kitchen when the phone rang. Turning quickly, she ran back to the front hall, and lifted the extension on the table by the stairs.

As she did she heard a rattle at the door, and realized someone was home—it had to be either Strome or Kilty. She tucked back her hair and, facing the door, held the receiver to her ear.

She had barely said, "Hello," when Kyla's voice came on the line.

"Nairne, dear, is Kilty with you?"

"Just a sec…" Nairne heard the door handle turning, saw the door open. But it wasn't Kilty who appeared in the doorway a second later, it was Strome. She forced her lips into a smile, and gave a sketchy wave with her free hand. "Sorry, Kyla—someone was just coming in, and I wasn't sure if it was Kilty or Strome. It's Strome. But why are you asking if Kilty's here?" Nairne glanced at her watch. "He's at school—he doesn't come home for lunch——"

"He wasn't in school today——"

"Oh, he was, he set off early, but——"

"Nairne," Kyla interrupted gently, "he wasn't in school. Kevin just came home for lunch and he said that when he was on his way to school this morning he bumped into Kilty. The lad told Kevin life was too much of a hassle these days, he was sick of Glencraig, and he was taking off."

"Taking off? Running away, you mean?" Nairne's voice was faint. Automatically she looked toward Strome, who was hanging his black leather jacket in the cupboard, and she saw him freeze for a second, before jerking his head around to look at her. Their eyes locked, and she saw the shock in his. She knew it must mirror her own.

"Where was he going? Did he give Kevin any clue?"

"That was all he said, but you know how curious Kevin is—he followed Kilty a little way. Nairne, he didn't take the main road out of town—he...went along the track leading up to Slagmhor."

Nairne felt a cold chill clutch her heart. "Slagmhor? You mean he's gone up to the peak?"

"I think so. Oh, I wish Adam were here. He knows the mountain like the back of his hand, he'd go after him...but he won't be home from Edinburgh till tomorrow..."

"Oh, dear Lord..." Nairne felt all the color draining from her face. "It'll be freezing cold up there—all that snow!—and you know he never wears anything but that damned kilt. What am I——?"

She wasn't allowed to finish what she'd been going to say. Strome had crossed the hall in three long strides, and before she could anticipate his action he'd taken the phone from her.

"Mrs. Garvie?" His voice was hard, and brusque. "You don't have to worry about the boy. I'll look after things. Nairne will phone you once I've found him."

As he replaced the receiver Nairne realized that she was trembling. It was, of course, reaction to the news that Kilty had run away. But it was also reaction to

Strome's high-handed manner. Anger bubbled up inside her, and as she stood glaring up at him, her hands clenched into fists, the anger boiled over in the form of raging, accusing words.

"What do you think you're doing?" she blazed. "Who gave you the right to grab the phone like that, to cut in on a private conversation about——?"

But, even as she castigated him, Nairne realized that perhaps, in this case, he *did* have a right. With a great effort she jerked on the reins of her self-control. He had, possibly, more of a right than she to be concerned...

He was the boy's father.

In the heat of the moment, in her distress, she had briefly forgotten that important fact. If anyone should be worried, if anyone should step forward and take charge of the situation, it should be Strome.

"I'm sorry," she said huskily. "I didn't mean to be so——"

"That's all right." He rubbed his hand distractedly across his nape. "This...Slagmhor? You think he's gone there... Tell me about it."

Nairne hugged her arms around herself, feeling icy, despite the warm air in the hall. "It's the mountain you can see from your bedroom window. In summer, in fine weather, it makes a good climb. Kilty loves it—he used to take his camera and a backpack in the summer holidays and spend days at a time up there, camping, taking pictures——"

"This isn't summer." Strome's voice was harsh. "It's the middle of winter, for pity's sake." He raked a hand through his hair distraughtly. "I'm going after him."

"You can't! You don't know the way——"

"There are trails, aren't there? I'll find him."

"I'm coming with you——"

"No!"

"You can't stop me." Nairne no longer felt the panic that had been shaking her a few moments ago. An icy calm had descended over her, an icy calm that steadied her mind and made things crystal clear. "And I can help you. I've known Slagmhor since I was a child, and if he's up there I'll know where to look for him. There are bothies on the mountain—rough huts for climbers to shelter in——"

"I know what bothies are," he said tersely. "I may live in the city but that doesn't make me a moron." He muttered a low, intense oath, and then, after a moment, said grimly, "Sorry. That was uncalled for. All right, you may have a point. It won't do anyone any good if I get lost."

"We'll need to take some things with us," Nairne said, trying to sound brisk, positive. "Warm clothes for Kilty, a first-aid kit, three sleeping bags, in case—heaven forbid—we can't get down before darkness sets in. I'll get two packsacks ready." She gestured dismissively toward Strome's black leather shoes, which had been fashioned for walking city pavements. "You can't wear those. If you go out the kitchen door you'll find a shed in the garden—there's a pile of steel-toed boots on a shelf, boots that the boys use when they're working around Bruach. I'm sure you'll find a pair that'll fit. I'll put a pair of wool socks in your room, and a down jacket—you'll need them."

"How long will it take you to get ready?"

"About fifteen minutes. First I have to call the police and let them know what's happened. In the circumstances, they may decide to contact the Glencraig Mountain Rescue Team. In any event, they should know that we're going up the mountain after Kilty."

"I'll phone. What's the number?"

"In the kitchen—you'll find a list by the phone——"

He started off for the kitchen even before she'd finished speaking. Feeling strangely unreal, Nairne whirled around and ran quickly up the stairs. If only Adam had been home—he'd climbed Slagmhor many times and in all weather; she'd have felt so much more confident had he been the one going with her. Strome—oh, he was anxious, and determined, true enough...but he was, after all, a city man. He would probably be a hindrance, rather than a help.

Tugging open her bedroom cupboard, she hauled out her warmest parka and heaviest woolen pants, and then burrowed away into the corner to find her hiking boots. As she did so an image of Kilty forced itself into her head, an image of him shivering in his thin T-shirt, with his bare legs white with cold...

"Oh, dear God," she whispered, "let us find him. Let us find him..."

But, even as she murmured the anguished words, she was rummaging wildly in a drawer for her warmest sweater. Prayers were fine, she knew, but much more powerful and effective when they were accompanied by positive action. And, besides, there wasn't a moment to waste. She and Strome had to find Kilty before it got dark. The mountains were cruel, and without mercy, to those who didn't give them the respect they deserved.

CHAPTER EIGHT

"LET'S stop here for a moment." Panting, Nairne slid her packsack off and dropped it on a clump of heather at the side of the narrow trail. "Time for a breather."

Strome planted one booted foot on a granite rock and, fingers curved around the straps of his packsack, gazed down into the glen, back the way they'd come. "What beautiful country this is." His tone was awed... almost reverent.

Drawing in a deep lungful of the sharp, clean air, Nairne followed the flight of two ravens flying overhead, their familiar "Chronk! Chronk!" call echoing in the stillness. "Yes," she said, "Scotland's the most beautiful country on earth."

She was aware that he had turned his head and was looking down at her. "You sound pretty sure of that." There was a faintly mocking edge to his tone. "You've seen a bit of the world, have you—you've got something solid on which to base that very definite statement?"

"No, I haven't traveled much. I went on a bus tour of the continent years ago with my parents, but that's all..."

"That's it?" He sounded surprised. "You've no desire to travel?"

Nairne shrugged, as if she could take it or leave it. She could have told him the truth... but then she'd have felt guilty, as if somehow she were betraying Rory. She *would* have liked to travel. She'd had a dream, once, to go for a holiday with him to some tropical paradise where the sun shone every day, and there were palm trees, and exotic birds, and flowers she'd never seen before... But Rory had said he wouldn't be comfortable in a place like that—and besides, he'd added jokingly, there were so

many places in Scotland he'd never seen and he wanted
to see them all before he died.

He hadn't, as it had turned out, seen them all. But
he had seen many of them. They had seen them together.
And for that Nairne was thankful. Thankful, too, that
she hadn't insisted on having her own way.

"*You've* traveled a lot, I take it?" she said.

"A fair bit."

Now that they had stopped walking, Nairne realized
just how icy cold the wind was at this higher altitude.
They had been climbing steadily for more than an hour,
and as she turned and squinted against the sun at the
path ahead, followed its curving way up the side of the
mountain, she saw that in another twenty minutes or so
they would reach the snow line. There had so far been
no sign of Kilty. But once they reached the snow surely
they would see his prints...if, indeed, this was the way
he had come.

He had to have come this way. They would find him
in the next half hour, sheltering in the first bothy.

She would not allow any negative thoughts to enter
her head.

She tried to force her mind into other channels. "When
you said the glen was beautiful a moment ago," she
murmured, "there was something in your voice...oh,
I'm maybe being fanciful...but it sounded to me as if
you have a real affinity for this country. You've told me
you were born in Manchester, but, with a name like
Strome Galbraith, surely you're at least part Scottish."

"Not part Scottish—a hundred percent, apart from
the accident of having been born in England. My father
came from the Loch Lomond area, and my mother from
a place in Sutherland called Strome—or so I believe."

Nairne stared at him. "So you...believe? Don't you
know?"

"She ran out on my father after I was born—left me
with him. He wouldn't talk about her. I learned never
to mention her name. He died when I was twenty, but

from the time I was old enough to listen he instilled in me his belief that women were not to be trusted.'' He laughed grimly. "And why would I have doubted him? The evidence was there . . . my own mother had deserted me . . ."

Ah, now Nairne knew why he'd seemed upset when she had asked him if his mother had taught him not to be vain. His mother hadn't been around to teach him anything. But her *absence* had taught him something . . . something that had cruelly slanted his attitude toward women. All women.

"And the one time I threw caution to the winds,'' he was continuing bitterly, "the one time I decided to trust——''

He broke off, but he didn't need to say any more. He must, of course, be referring to his affair with Hazel.

And was this why he had finally come for his son? Had he finally realized that by not claiming him he was as guilty of desertion as his mother had been?

"About Kilty——'' she swallowed to get rid of a sudden tightness in her throat "—what will you do with him? Will he travel with you, or will you put him in boarding school?''

She hadn't turned back to Strome while she asked the question, not wanting him to see the shine of tears in her eyes. She'd kept her blurred gaze fixed on the peak above, the snow a glimmering white sheet with its crystals dancing blue, red, green, purple in the sun's rays. But when he didn't answer she blinked back the tears and turned around.

He wasn't, however, looking at her.

He was still staring down into the valley, like a statue carved from the mountainside, except for the strands of thick black hair flying around his forehead.

"Kilty,'' she said again, anxiety making her voice harsh, brusque, "when you take him, will you——?''

"I heard you the first time.''

"Then why didn't you answer?" Nairne roughly drew her own wind-tossed hair back from her cheeks and glowered at his granite-hard profile. "And, if you don't want to answer, at least have the decency to acknowledge that you——"

"You want an answer?" He twisted around as he spoke, and Nairne almost cringed from him when she saw the expression on his face. His eyes were as bleak and wintry as the day. "I'll give you an answer, then. No, I won't take my son traveling with me—nor will I put him in boarding school——"

"But what other alternative——?"

"—I shall leave him in Glencraig, Mrs. Campbell, and his life will go on just as it would have, had I never discovered his existence. You talked about adopting him—I have no objections. I'll make sure he's taken care of financially. And he'll inherit my estate after my death."

Was it the high altitude? Nairne wondered confusedly. Was it lack of oxygen that was making her brain so dull? She should be able to understand what he was saying, but it didn't make sense. It sounded, she thought with a shake of her head, as if he wanted to return to the city and leave Kilty in Glencraig. Oh, dear Lord . . .

"Yes, Nairne," Strome's voice was weary, "you're not mistaken in what you think you heard. When I return to London I shall return alone." He reached down and picked up her packsack, and held it out to her. Slowly she lifted her gloved hands to grasp it, but as she took hold of the leather straps his own grip tightened, and when she made to take it from him he didn't let it go. She looked up, a jerky, questioning movement, and found herself staring into eyes that were as hard and pitiless as the granite hills around them.

"Every time I see that boy," he said, "I see his mother. Every time I think of that boy I *think* of his mother. And when I think of his mother there is a hatred that surges up inside me like a wellspring of poison, and that poison spills over to her son——"

"I don't know what Hazel could have done to warrant your unforgiving feelings," Nairne cried, "but Kilty's done nothing to deserve such harshness!" There were tears in her voice. "For the love of God, Strome, don't turn from him—he's your *son*!"

He didn't answer. As if her plea had fallen on totally deaf ears, he turned away from her and began trudging up the steep slope. His shoulders were slumped, as if the weight of the whole world were on his shoulders.

Her gaze blurred, Nairne wrenched her packsack on and, tugging the straps into place, hurried to catch up with him. She could only imagine what he must be feeling, but she sensed that he was being torn apart inside. Because of his hatred of Hazel he was trying not to become emotionally involved with his son. It was obvious that he was finding the struggle a hard one. She had thought in the beginning that, whatever was troubling him, she might be able to help. Now she knew she was wrong. Only he could free himself of the bitterness that was consuming him.

Only he could undo the shackles binding his heart and set it free.

At the top of Slagmhor was a cairn, a pile of rough stones built into a mound over the years by those climbers who had added a rock to the ones already there, as a testament to their achievement in conquering the peak. On this wild winter afternoon the cairn was shrouded in snow.

Nairne stood with her back to it, hunched against the howling wind. The sun, low in the sky during the afternoon at this time of year, had gone down a while ago, the sky had turned gray, the mountains shadowed, the glen dark and distant. Her body felt chilled to the bone. She felt an aching shudder rake through her as she looked up at Strome.

"He's not here," she called despairingly, her words torn away almost before she'd uttered them. "He's not on the mountain."

"He couldn't have gone down the other side?"

"It's not possible," she shouted, "to go down that way. There's a very steep cliff, and at the foot of it there's MacDiarmid's Gully..." She swallowed. She'd been trying not to think about the gully. But, if Kilty had decided to try that way, there was no point in looking for him. The gully was hundreds of feet deep...

She caught her breath as a blast of wind almost choked her, and she pulled her scarf up over her mouth. "We'd best be getting back. It'll soon be dark..."

As she called out the muffled words she looked up at the sky, and felt dismay flood through her. "Oh, Lord," she whispered, "it's going to snow again. But the weatherman said..."

Her voice trailed away as an extra-strong gust of wind howled past, whirling thousands of tiny snowflakes around them, so that for a mind-freezing moment she couldn't see Strome. She was alone, away up here, miles from anywhere...

Then his hard fingers were gripping her arm. "When did you ever know the weatherman to be anything but wrong?" His voice was grim. "Looks as if we're in for a blizzard. We'd better hightail it for shelter before we get lost. And don't worry about Kilty. He's more than likely thought better of his impetuous decision to run away, and is probably back in Bruach, sitting by a warm fire."

He might well be right, Nairne thought as she scrambled down over the snow-covered rocks, supported by Strome's strong hand. Kilty might not actually be sitting by a warm fire...but he certainly wasn't on Slagmhor. They'd have spotted him by now. Yes, he might have been there earlier; she and Strome had seen tracks in the snow around the door of the first bothy on their way up, and around the door of the second, too, when they had come to it. But the wind was so wild, the snow so featherlight, that it hadn't been possible to tell if they were human footprints or tracks of a mountain hare.

Both bothies had been empty. The smaller one, close to the summit, was just a hut, offering nothing but shelter to a traveler caught by darkness or a sudden storm. The other one, which they would be passing again in about twenty minutes on their way down, had once been a shepherd's cottage, the room in front having a roughly hewn fireplace. The room at the back had been quite bare, but Nairne had noticed in the larger room a pile of birch logs and a few kindlers in a corner, and a dirty-looking pallet angled against the far wall, a filthy blanket tossed over it. Behind the outside door was a broken whisky bottle, entwined in cobwebs, and, littering the stone floors, bags and paper tossed down by careless hikers. Certainly not the Hilton, she'd reflected wryly as she'd pulled the creaking wooden door closed again...but, then again, anyone forced to spend the night there would not be in any position to be choosy...

With every minute that passed it was getting harder to stand upright against the force of the gale; it was getting harder to breathe, harder to see. The snowflakes were getting thicker and thicker, more and more clinging. Already Strome's black hair was white-capped, his eyebrows the same. But, despite the merciless wind that buffeted them with unabated fury, as if determined to fling them off the face of the mountain, his movements down the rough trail were powerful and confident. And to Nairne they looked almost effortless.

She'd been wrong about him, she found herself thinking.

"I must apologize to you." Her breathing was ragged with her effort to keep up with him. "I was mistaken..."

"About what?"

"I thought—since you're a city man—that you'd be a——"

"A wimp?" The amusement in his voice was genuine. "You thought you'd leave me behind after the first few hundred yards, and——"

"More or less." Nairne lost her balance as she jumped down from a huge rock, and as she twisted aound he caught her and lifted her to safety. "Thanks," she said, and felt her cheeks flush as he held her for a moment longer than necessary, with the wind whipping around his head, lifting away some of the snow and whisking it away. "Why... why are you looking at me like that?" she asked, almost in a whisper, as she found herself trapped in his gaze.

"Your hair," he said softly, "it's white—covered in snow. I caught just a flashing glimpse, as I looked down at you, of how you'd look fifty years from now: your face still enchantingly lovely, your nose still dusted with cinnamon freckles, your lips still full and satin smooth——" He stopped short. "It's not the right time for this, is it?" His mouth twisted in a smile, and she saw warmth deep in his eyes, and knew that the smile was real, and from the heart. "But there will be a time, and it will be soon." Her scarf had slipped down, and before he started moving again he gently pulled it up and tightened it, so it once again protected the lower part of her face.

Feeling as dizzy as if she'd been whirling on a merry-go-round, Nairne floundered through the snow beside him, hardly aware that her pants now soaked, her legs wet, and the tops of her boots chafing against her skin. She was cold, she was weary, she knew she must look like a walking snowman. And she had probably never in her life been in such a precarious situation before—clambering down a mountain in the middle of winter, in a snowstorm that was becoming more terrifying by the moment. And yet—the realization stunned her—there was no one with whom she would rather be.

What was it about this man, this city man, that made her feel safe?

Safe—and yet at the same time in very grave danger, because when she was with him she felt a stirring inside her, deep in her soul. He touched her as no one else ever had. And she knew that, with every minute they spent together, he came closer to stealing a piece of her heart.

"There it is!" Nairne's voice was hoarse as she cried out the words. "Oh, I can't believe it! Thank heavens..."

It was, she knew, a miracle that they'd found the second bothy; she'd never before experienced such a complete whiteout. Her eyes were pained with the glare of it, her face stinging with the sleeting onslaught of it. As they'd stumbled down the mountainside, she clinging to Strome's jacket, he grasping her in an unbreakable grip, time had ceased to exist. Nothing had existed but the blizzard screaming around them, as if furiously raging at them that they had no business to be there. She could have sworn they'd been fighting their way down the rugged, treacherous slope for an hour, but it must have been less, for here they were, at the bothy. Shelter at last. No Hilton, she acknowledged, raking up the last vestiges of her humor as she recalled her earlier thoughts on the matter.

The door creaked as Strome shoved it open, and, as he pulled her inside, a wild sweep of snow flurried in with them. Strome rammed the door shut again, and they stood together in the dark, not speaking, Nairne huddled against the powerful figure beside her, listening to the now slightly muffled but still terrifying inferno of the storm.

"We're here for the night." Strome's voice was quiet.

"Yes," Nairne whispered, "I'm afraid we are. But," she went on, trying to sound hopeful, confident, "in the morning, if the storm passes, we should be able to get back. At least the police know where we are, if——"

"Let's not dwell on the 'if's, Nairne." She heard him take in a deep breath. "What we must do is take care of the here and now. And the first thing to do is get warm."

Nairne heard the strength in his words, and she tried to take strength from them, but now that they were no longer walking she could feel the shivering start. "Right," her words came out in a shudder, "I noticed some logs and kindlers earlier, in the corner. We must try to get a fire going. I brought matches, of course, and I've a flashlight too. I didn't think we'd need it—it was a last-minute idea."

"And a damned good one. Here, let me help you take your backpack off." She felt his warm breath on her cold cheeks as he twisted the pack over her shoulders, before letting it drop to the floor.

Nairne fumbled for a moment with the buckle closure, and then, with an exasperated exclamation, peeled off her sodden gloves and stuffed them in her jacket pocket. Undoing the pack with numbed fingers, she took out the lightweight flashlight, and flicked it on. Its thin beam wavered around in the darkness, before she aimed it into the corner where she'd seen the birch logs.

"There," she said as Strome shrugged off his packsack, "and—I never thought the day would come when I'd say this—thank goodness for litterbugs." After shaking the snow from her hair, and brushing it from her jacket, she gathered up the discarded paper bags and cardboard containers from the stone floor. "We have all the makings for a good fi——" She broke off abruptly as she heard what sounded like a groan behind her. "What happened? Have you hurt yourself?"

"No," Strome's voice was tense, "I'm all right. Here, give me that flashlight for a moment..."

Nairne held out the flashlight and he took it. Biting her lip, she watched as he flashed it around in the darkness. Over the door, up over the ceiling, across the walls, over the floor...

"Oh, dear Lord..." Nairne felt dizzy, as if all the blood had drained away from her body. In the pencil-thin light from the flashlight she had seen... No, it couldn't be——

"Get the fire going, Nairne." Strome's voice was harsher than she'd ever heard it. "I'll get him into a sleeping bag. We have to get him warmed up."

It was Kilty. He was lying on the dirty pallet, his only covering the ragged blanket. He was curled up in the fetal position, his eyes closed, his face white as the snow whirling outside, his body shaking as if he had malaria.

He must have been hiding behind the mattress when they'd looked in earlier, Nairne thought dully. He must have heard them approach, and hurried to conceal himself. He could never have guessed they'd have to come back to the bothy again; he'd have thought he was safe——

"Nairne! Snap out of it!" Strome shook her arm roughly. "Get the fire going."

How she got herself to move, Nairne didn't know, but somehow she did. And somehow in the near pitch-dark she managed to find her waterproof matches, managed to gather up an armful of logs and take them to the rough hearth. It was almost as if someone else was in her body, the actions carried out as if she were on automatic pilot. When bright flames crackled the paper, when the kindling caught hold right away, and the yellow tongues licked the birch bark, leaping instantly up the throat of the chimney, she watched, mesmerized, as if she were watching the whole thing on film. Only when the warmth glowed against her chilled cheeks did she finally find her frozen thoughts begin to thaw.

And, as she looked around, it was to see, in the fire's flickering light, that Strome had managed to get Kilty into one of the sleeping bags, had zipped it up and had pulled the pallet close to the hearth. He had taken off the lad's wet Reeboks and socks and was arranging them by the fire.

"How is he?" Her words came out chokingly, as if someone had her in a stranglehold. "Is he going to be all right?"

CHAPTER NINE

STROME turned, and in the erratic flickering of the fire-light Nairne saw that his face was drawn into haggard lines. But his voice was steady as he said, "Yes, he's going to be all right. He must have holed up in here before the blizzard—though his footwear's soaked through, the rest of his clothes are dry. He's cold and exhausted, that's all. Had we not found him it would, of course, be a different matter..."

Relief surged through Nairne—along with other emotions, emotions that shook her with their intensity, emotions that were as stormy, as turbulent, as unpredictable as the blizzard raging outside. Was she crazy, that, even in a situation such as this, she couldn't keep her eyes off the man who was now getting up from his crouching position by the pallet? Bulky in his down parka, with his lean face gaunt, his eyes dark pools of unhappiness, he drew her to him inexorably. Oh, part of it was pity, she acknowledged that freely; pity, because she knew he was suffering. Pain was his companion, a companion he didn't want, but a companion who ruthlessly, cruelly hounded him, had been hounding him for fifteen years...

A companion created by Hazel.

How he must have loved her, that he could have been so wounded by her. To have been so poisoned by...whatever it was she had done——

He came to her side, and looked down at the fire. "You brought food?"

"Cheese and oatcakes. A couple of bars of chocolate and some nuts. But you're not going to try to waken him, are you? He's——"

128

"Not for Kilty. For us." Without taking his gaze from the fire, he put an arm around her shoulder and drew her against his chest. "It's hours since we've eaten. It's going to be a long night. We should have something—we have to keep our strength up—but we'll eke out our supplies. Who knows how long we may be trapped here?"

He didn't go on, and Nairne felt suddenly even more chilled than she had been when she was outside in the freezing cold. She'd closed her mind to the possibility that the storm might go on for days; to have that possibility put into words conjured up all sorts of pictures that——

"Are you wet through?"

Strome's question, thankfully, broke into her thoughts. "My socks are damp, and my pants are wet from the thighs down, but under my jacket I'm okay. How about you?"

"Not so lucky." His face, alive with changing shadows as the firelight flickered over it, creased in a wry smile as he added, "I'm soaked. Let's get the wet things off, then. I'll arrange them on logs in front of the hearth. They should be dried out by morning."

"We'll get into our sleeping bags now?"

"That's the idea."

Nairne stood for a moment, watching as Strome unzipped his parka and shrugged it off. She could tell by the leaden way it hung that it was saturated, and it was no surprise when she saw that his sweater clung to his torso like a second skin. But it did take her by surprise when, without any further ado, he ripped it off. One minute he was standing before her fully clothed, the next his chest was revealed to her startled gaze in all its dark-haired muscular glory.

She was too late to stifle the little sound that escaped her. He heard it, and looked down at her. Their eyes met, and she saw, to her embarrassment, that his were gleaming with amusement.

"I . . . g-guess I'd better get my wet things off too."
Cheeks bright pink, Nairne turned her back on him and
took her jacket off, before starting on her pants. The
button at the waistband had never been so hard to open,
but finally she wrenched it from the buttonhole. The
sound of the zip coming down was, to her mind, so
suggestive that she found herself digging her teeth painfully into her lower lip. It seemed to take forever to get
the wet fabric pulled down over her thighs, but finally,
after a struggle, she did, and only then did she realize
she still had her boots on.

As she untied the leather laces and tugged her boots
off she could hear small sounds behind her, the sound
of clothing being removed, and her throat tightened.
When she had to face him again, as face him she undoubtedly must, what was she going to see? He was
already naked from the waist up——

"Here," his voice came from behind her as she slid
her pants off, "give those to me."

Without looking around, she handed over her jacket,
her pants and her socks. Then, crouching down in her
sweater and underpants, she pulled her sleeping bag out
from her packsack. Still without looking around, she
unzipped it, but before she could step into the bag she
felt a steady hand on her shoulder.

"Uh, uh," he said.

She twisted her head around.

"It'll be warmer," he went on, "if we zip them
together——"

"No!" Her gasp was indignant. How could he suggest
such a thing? "We can't do that!"

"Why not?" One dark eyebrow rose quizzically.
"Aren't the zips . . . compatible?"

"Oh, yes, the sleeping bags are compatible—the zips
will fit—it's just that——"

"So the zips are compatible . . . and we are compatible, so——"

"I just can't."

"Look, Nairne," Strome shoved his damp hair back from his forehead, "I don't know what kind of a sex maniac you think I am, but I certainly am not going to try to have my way with you—sweet and tempting though that thought is!—in this place and at this time, with a teenage boy just feet away...no matter how out of it he may be at the moment. Okay?"

"Yes," Nairne muttered. "I know. You're only being practical. Sorry for being stupid about it."

She lowered her head, and felt a shudder ripple through her as she saw for the first time that he was absolutely naked except for a pair of close-fitting white briefs. A huge lump rose in her throat, almost closing it. His body was magnificent. Powerful, muscular, and tanned, with the same rough growth of hair on his arms and his legs as was on his chest. In the space of an instant the walls of the bothy seemed to close in on her, so that nothing existed except for this man, his physical presence, a presence that, despite his reassuring words of a moment ago, was threatening, dangerous...and sensually, wildly, erotically disturbing. Her pulse was racing out of control, in unison with her frantically charging heartbeats. She couldn't just keep staring at his body...but there was only one other way to go and that was up.

She looked up.

His eyes were dark. "You may look, Mrs. Campbell, but you may not touch."

"I don't want to t——"

A hard fingertip was placed gently but firmly over her trembling lips. "Yes, you do want to touch." The smoky eyes held a touch of self-derision as he allowed them to slide down over the swell of her full breasts, over her slender hips and over her bare legs. "Just as I do. I think, in the interests of all concerned, we should, after all, each sleep in our own sleeping bag——"

Nairne wrenched her face away from his fingertip. "That's what I wanted in the first place," she hissed.

"Now will you kindly get yourself into yours, and stop displaying yourself like some . . . some male stripper, and I'll get into mine and get us something to eat?"

She knew he was watching her as she spread out her bag and got into it, knew he was still watching her as she pulled her packsack over beside her and started taking out the food. Not until she had given him time to get into his own sleeping bag and had heard him pull up the long zip did she let her eyes rest on him again.

He wasn't lying down, as she'd expected, but was sitting up in the bag, having pulled the upper part of it around his wide shoulders, his hands stretched out to the fire. He must have sensed that she was looking at him, because he turned around.

"Shadow," he said softly. "He was in the kitchen when we left. Who's going to let him out?"

Nairne wriggled to a sitting position too, hauling her bag over her shoulders like a shawl. How astonishing, that he should have been thinking of Shadow, obviously concerned about him. Handing him a slice of moist cheddar cheese and a thick homemade oatcake, she said, "I phoned Kate—my mother—before we left, while you were upstairs changing. She's going to keep an eye on him till we get back."

"Good." He didn't say any more for a minute or two while they ate, and then he asked, "How long have you had him?"

"Shadow? Eight years. He was a wedding present from Kevin."

"From your nephew? Your sister must have married a few years before you did, then——"

"Oh, no. We had a double wedding—Kyla and Adam, Rory and I. A grand affair, in the parish kirk!"

The smell of the wood smoke permeated the air, as did the crackling of the fire, as Strome said, after a short pause, "But Kevin—I thought he was eleven or twelve——"

Nairne grimaced. "He's twelve. Sorry, I should have explained—Adam isn't Kevin's natural father. Kyla was married before, to a boy she'd known all her life, Drew Ferguson. They eloped and emigrated to Canada, and Kevin was born in Toronto. Drew died when Kevin was four, and Kyla brought her son back to the glen. She married Adam a short time later, and settled here."

"So Garvie's her second husband," Strome said, a faint edge of surprise in his voice. "They seem very happy."

"They were made for each other," Nairne said simply.

"Made for each other..." Strome's lips twisted in a cynical smile. "You really believe that two people can be made for each other? Twin souls...?"

Nairne nibbled the last crumbs of her oatcake, savoring it. Who knew when they'd eat next? "Yes," she said, nodding firmly, "I do believe that two people can be made for each other... that they can be what you call... twin souls."

"But if someone falls in love and marries more than once... surely that invalidates your premise? Or can a person have more than one twin soul floating about in the world... perhaps a triplet soul?"

He was teasing her, she knew... but she also knew that he really wanted an answer to his question. Could she give him one?

"No," she said quietly, staring into the flames, "I don't believe in triplet souls. But I do believe that a person can find a soul mate, someone who complements him or her, so that when they meet their coming together makes a perfect whole."

"Do you think Kyla and Drew were soul mates?"

Normally Nairne wouldn't have discussed Kyla in an intimate fashion with anyone, but there was something about Strome that made her powerless to deny him the answers he wanted.

"No." Her voice was a whisper. "No, they weren't soul mates. Drew was crazy about Kyla, and Kyla did love him, but not in the same way. They had always been good friends, and she loved him the way one does love a good friend. But with Adam it was different. With him she learned the real meaning of love—love between a man and a woman. Adam is her soul mate.''

"Two equal parts coming together to make a perfect whole... like you and your Rory.''

She didn't move her gaze from the fire; she knew he was looking at her, and she didn't want him to see the expression in her eyes. Didn't want him to see the tears glimmering—tears that had welled there as a great giant hand had squeezed her heart so that she could scarcely bear the pain. Pain that had been caused by his softly spoken words—his innocently spoken words. Pain that had almost made her cry out aloud as she faced the harsh truth, the unpalatable truth, the truth that pierced her to the core: though she had loved Rory and he had loved her, they hadn't been twin souls. They had worked together in harmony, they had played together in harmony, they had made love together in harmony. And their love had been gentle, unselfish, sharing... But something had been missing——

Oh, she hadn't known it at the time. And, had she never met Strome Galbraith, in all likelihood she would never have known it. Would never have known that when she and Rory had come together they had not been two equal parts of a perfect whole. They had not been soul mates.

What had been missing from their relationship was passion.

The wild, fierce passion that she now knew she was capable of, this fire in the blood, this deep craving, this need——

She felt herself tremble as Strome's warm fingers touched her jaw, cupping it tenderly and drawing her around to face him. She wanted to resist, and perhaps five minutes ago she could have, but not now, now when she was still reeling, dizzy and confused, over her new and devastating discovery.

"You're crying!" There was shock in Strome's husky voice. "Oh, Nairne..."

He drew her close, and as her sleeping bag slid down over her back he wrapped his own around her so that she was cradled in his arms, warm, loved...

Loved? No, not loved. How foolish to think he could love her. He of the cold, bitter heart.

"I'm sorry," he murmured, his lips brushing her ear, "I made you think of Rory. I upset you. What a brute I——"

Even as she heard the remorse in his voice, she found herself whispering, "No, don't feel like that—you're wrong, that's not why I'm crying."

"Then...why?" Tender hands caressed her arm, gentle fingers wound their way through her damp hair. "Tell me..."

How could she tell him? How could she tell him that she was crying because she felt an aching sense of loss now when she thought of her marriage—an emptiness—that filled her with sorrow? How could she tell him that in her heart she thanked God she hadn't met him while she was married to Rory, for she would have been inexorably drawn to him, despite her instinctive knowlege that she should keep her distance, just as a child was inexplicably drawn to the dangers of deep water——?

"Sometimes it helps to talk." He smoothed her hair back gently, ran a fingertip down the curved line of her cheekbone. "When you bring it out into the——"

He broke off abruptly as Nairne closed her eyes on a shuddering indrawn breath.

"What is it?" he asked tensely. "What's wrong?"

You're what's wrong, she wanted to cry, you're what's wrong. Why do I feel this way when you touch me? Why do I feel as if I've known you all my life...and why do I feel as if I want to spend the rest of my life right here, in your embrace?

But she didn't say the words. Never would say the words. "I'm sorry," she said in a low voice, unsteadily. "I don't know what's wrong—I guess all this excitement today has just been too much for me. I think it's time to call it a night." She slid from under the warm protection of his shoulder, and, adjusting her own sleeping bag, pushed herself down into it. Twisting herself around so that she had her back to him, she made herself as comfortable as was possible, considering the hard floor and her freezing feet.

For a time that seemed endlessly long there was no sound from Strome. Then, finally, she heard scuffling noises, and guessed that he, too, was making himself comfortable.

"See you in the morning," she murmured.

There was no answer, and, frowning, she twisted around and peered across at him . . . to see that he was not lying in his bag, as she'd expected him to be, but crouched over by Kilty's pallet. He had his palm on his son's forehead. And his whole attitude was one of caring, of concern.

Quietly she twisted away from him so that he wouldn't see her watching him. For some unaccountable reason, she felt like crying again. What an enigmatic man he was, complex, impossible to understand. One thing was sure—no matter how hard he appeared on the surface, no matter how determined he was not to get involved with his son, there was a tenderness inside him that he had, unwittingly, revealed to her eyes. Nairne was sure that, though he had said he didn't want Kilty, the struggle inside him must be intensifying as he looked at this young lad who had been formed in his image, of his flesh and blood.

A moment later she heard the sound of his movements, heard him pull up his zip. "Good night, Nairne." His voice was low, husky, tentative. He obviously wasn't sure if she was still awake or not.

She exhaled in a gentle breath, "Good night, Strome."
She smiled, even though tears were streaming uncontrollably down her cheeks. "See you in the morning."

Surprisingly, she slept.

When she awoke, and stared blearily at the luminous
hands of her watch, she saw to her astonishment that it
was almost eight. And as she gradually came to herself
she discovered what must have wakened her. Strome—
fully dressed again—was adding logs to the fire, and they
were sparking and crackling loudly.

He must have kept the blaze going all night, because
the bothy was warm. Not only warm, but almost cozy,
Nairne found herself thinking, with the shadows dancing
against the walls...so different from the way it had
looked yesterday in the hard light of day when she'd
looked in, so distraught, hoping to see Kilty...

Kilty.

She jerked her head around and peered across at the
figure lying on the pallet. He was no longer curled up
in a ball; she could see by his outline that he was sprawled
out as much as was possible in the confines of the
sleeping bag. He was lying on his back and he was
snoring gently.

Nairne felt herself relax, felt a strange sense of peace
flow through her. Strome had been right—Kilty was fine.
But if Kevin hadn't followed to see where he was going
yesterday morning——

Firmly, Nairne cut off that train of thought, and concentrated on the gentle rhythm of his snoring and the
reassuring sizzle of the fire. The two sounds were, she
suddenly noticed, the only ones she could hear. The
storm—oh, thank heavens, the storm had abated. Soon
they'd be able to start down the mountain again...

"You're awake." Strome's voice was just a murmur.
"Sleep well?" He crouched down beside her.

"Mm, yes, I did...and feel more than a little guilty
for not taking a shift during the night."

"Shift?"

She gestured toward the flames leaping up the chimney. "Keeping the home fires burning," she said softly. "We'd all have been shivering in the dark if you hadn't——"

"You were exhausted. Emotionally and physically. I wouldn't have wakened you for the world—in fact, it was good to hear you snoring——"

"*Snoring*?"

Kilty muttered a protesting groan at the sound of her indignant squeal, and as she glanced quickly at him she saw him turn onto his side, his eyes still closed. "I *never* snore!" she hissed under her breath, but before she could say more Strome's lean face creased in a grin.

"Just checking," he said smoothly. "I always find it best to, when I'm planning to sleep with someone."

While he was speaking he had made himself comfortable on top of his sleeping bag, and now he was lying alongside her, looking down at her, his head propped up on his hand, his eyes twinkling with mischief as he waited for her response.

Her response...

Nairne was thankful that he could have no idea of her response—her body's response, her heart's response. When he looked at her like that, his eyes so warm and beguiling, she felt as if he were drawing her very soul from her. This was a man she could willingly die for; he was everything a man should be, and so very much more. She was utterly helpless when she was close to him—if he reached out now and took her in his arms she would have been unable to resist him...

Was this how Hazel had felt when he'd looked at her?

The thought was like a slashing wound to the heart. Why did it hurt so, to think of him with Hazel?

"Were you in love with her?" she whispered.

How strange it was, almost as if he'd read her mind, as if he'd followed her thought processes. He knew immediately what she was talking about, whom she was talking about. His face sobered, and he fell back on his sleeping bag, hands clasped behind his head, his eyes closed.

"Yes," he said wearily after a long, long silence, "I was in love with her. It was like a sweet dream...a dream that turned into a nightmare."

His dark hair, she noticed for the first time, had a cowlick that made it curl over on to his forehead when it was dry, the way it was now. She was overcome by an irresistible impulse to reach over, and smooth it down.

His hair was silky soft to her gentle touch, and the feel of it against her fingertips made her heart ache. "Tell me about it," she said softly, propping her head with her hand and looking down, "about you and Hazel."

The fire was glowing with a dark red glow, and no longer sparked. Outside there was a sliding, thumping sound—snow falling off the roof. The only other sounds in the bothy as she waited were Kilty's even breathing and the beat of her own heart.

"I came to Scotland early that summer," he said in a low voice, "scouting for a piece of land. I'd just finished a project abroad, and with the skiing and tourist industry booming in the north I decided the time was right to invest in the area. And—because of my background, I guess—Scotland seemed to be pulling at me, like a magnet."

"What made you pick Glencraig?"

"The location was ideal. Close enough to the hills to be convenient, but comparatively un-Americanized, and far enough from the regular tourist stamping grounds to appeal to those who come north looking for the real Scotland—Scotland the way it used to be before everything became so commercialized. Craigend was...still is...perfect for my kind of setup."

Nairne shook her head. "But you didn't ever develop it. Why not?"

But she didn't need to see the almost imperceptible tightening of his lips to know the answer. Of course, it had to do with Hazel.

"I met her by chance." He grimaced, as if the very memory of that meeting was painful to him. "The day I found Craigend. I'd just been to see a property farther down the glen—it was no use, and I was feeling pretty disappointed, because I'd liked this general area right away. When I saw the ruins of the farmhouse at Craigend, and the obvious state of neglect around it, I wondered if it might be for sale. I parked by the roadside, and strolled through the fields. I became filled with excitement—the place was perfect. Bulldoze the house, the old steadings... Anyway, I was just standing there, dreaming, when this spirit appeared in front of me—a lovely Highland lass with a wild tumble of black hair, smoky green eyes and a husky, sensual chuckle that ensnared my senses..." He stopped short, as if, for a moment, he'd forgotten himself, and he laughed, a bitter laugh. "Of course, it was no spirit, it was a flesh and blood creature. But all the same, she enchanted me. 'What do you want here, city man?' she asked. And, 'I want you,' I replied. Love at first sight—corny, wasn't it? But it didn't seem corny at the time. She stole my heart."

"She loved you too?"

His jaw tightened. "She said she did. I thought she was footloose and fancy-free, and yet she always wanted to meet me somewhere quiet, private... After I'd known her for a couple of weeks she told me about...Hugh... about their understanding. She told me he was fishing, on the west coast, but she promised that when he came back at the end of June she'd tell him we were going to be married and break off with him." His chest lifted in a shuddering sigh. "On the last night of my trip we became lovers. And when I returned to London it was with the deeds to Craigend in my pocket...and, in my heart, Hazel Lindsay."

She thought he was going to stop there, and she couldn't bear not to know what had happened. But she didn't want to press—she could see how the memories tore at him——

"She wrote me." His tone was harsh. "When Hugh came back from the fishing she wrote and told me that the moment she saw him again she knew that he was the man she loved—that our affair had been a mistake, and it meant nothing to her. She said she didn't ever want to hear from me again—she and Hugh were going to be married right away."

A gentle wind sighed down the chimney, its current sending a small breath of smoky air into the bothy. Nairne blamed its faint pungency for the tears smarting behind her eyelids, but had nothing to blame for the ache in her heart, nothing but the compassion she felt for this man. He was telling the truth, she didn't doubt it. No one would have doubted it—it was there in his stark, hurting voice.

"I can almost forgive her for her lies," he went on tormentedly, "but I can never forgive her for not telling me she was pregnant. She should have told me. *I had a right to know*. Dear heaven, how could she have been so selfish...?"

The choking sob that filled the bothy was so anguished that for a brief, stunned moment Nairne thought it must have come from between her own lips. Certainly not from Strome's—for, just as it had been to her, the sound had been a surprise to him. His eyes were sharp and questioning...

The sob had come from Kilty.

He was lying on his stomach, hunched up, his head cradled in his arms. Dismay and horror coursed through Nairne. He hadn't been asleep; he must have heard everything. She couldn't see his face, but she could well imagine it. He had loved Hazel, and he had thought the world of Hugh...the man he had believed to be his father.

Now he knew he had been living with lies. This man, this stranger who had come into his life, was his father. And what a harsh way in which to discover something so shattering. And now he knew the truth about what had happened in the past, and it was probably tearing at him—just as it had torn at Strome, was still tearing at Strome.

"Oh, dear Lord," Nairne whispered through her tears, "oh, dear Lord."

Strome was on his feet, his face ravaged. "Bloody hell," his voice was tortured, "bloody hell—I never meant him to know——"

"I already knew . . . that you were my father." Kilty's voice was husky, muffled, pained. "I already knew. I was the one who——" He couldn't go on.

For a moment no one spoke, and then Strome whispered, slowly, as if he was stunned, "*You* were the one who hired the lawyer to trace me! I assumed it was your mother, before her death, who had set things in motion, for some reason . . . and I assumed also that she had kept the truth from you—that no one else knew Hugh wasn't your real father——"

"But where did you get the money, Kilty?" Nairne breathed out the question. "What little your parents left was barely enough to cover the funeral expenses."

"My camera."

"The camera." All of a sudden, things began to make sense to Nairne, and she felt a huge lump swell in her throat. "You sold your camera because you needed the money to hire a lawyer——"

"Oh, my God . . ." Remorse sent a spasm of pain across Strome's features. "That's why you said you *needed* it——"

"That's right," Kilty said quietly. "Not for drugs."

"I'm sorry. I know it's not enough, just saying that . . . but how can I take the words back? All I can say is that they were spoken out of concern for you."

"Aye." The boy sounded exhausted. "It's all right. I understand."

"What I don't understand," Strome stood over the figure hunched in the sleepingbag, "is why your mother finally decided to tell you the truth."

Kilty wrenched himself around and supported himself on his elbows as he stared up at Strome, his eyes drenched with tears. "Mam never told me. It was Dad—he told me about you in the hospital, before he died. Told me he wasn't my real father—confessed that he'd known all along. He said Mam never guessed that he knew. She never guessed that he'd sensed something different about her when he came back from the fishing that summer. And, when she found out not long after they were married that she was pregnant, she never knew Dad guessed her secret. Never guessed that he realized she must have had a lover while he was away at the fishing... and he loved her so much that he kept quiet all these years. The only thing Dad knew about the man... and it was more of a guess, he said... was that his name was Somerled——"

"Somerled?" Nairne's question was out before she could stop it. "But——"

Kilty jerked his head in Strome's direction and said huskily, "His middle name's Somerled—Mam always said it was just a name she liked."

Nairne felt the lump in her throat swell till it was so large that she could barely swallow. She certainly couldn't speak. All she could do was bite her trembling lip, and pray that she wouldn't give in to the tears that were welling up inside her. So much emotion... she could hardly bear it——

The bang on the bothy door was so loud, so unexpected, that she jumped. With a gasp she wrenched her head around, and was just in time to see the door opening, feel a gust of frigid, snow-sparkled air blow across her face. She screwed up her eyes against the brightness, and then a tall dark shape filled the doorway.

"Thank goodness you're all here," a familiar voice reached her ears, "and come to no harm, by the looks of you."

"Adam!" Forgetting that she was only half-dressed, Nairne lurched to her feet. "I thought you were in Edinburgh." She stumbled across the stone floor and threw her arms around her brother-in-law, oblivious to the feel of his chilly jacket against her body, the cold of the floor on her bare feet, and looked up into his face, which was ruddy from the icy morning air.

He hugged her tightly and smiled down at her. "I happened to phone Kyla just after she talked with you on the phone. She sounded so upset that I drove right home. We'd just organized a rescue party when the blizzard blew up, and we had to wait till it blew over. I can't tell you how relieved we were when we saw the smoke coming from the bothy chimney. Ah, Strome," Nairne was all at once aware that Strome was at her side, "you've made a good job of looking after these two. Congratulations. Not bad for a——"

"City man?" Strome's laugh was good-natured, and gave no sign of the tension he'd been under a few moments before. "You're not the only one who suspected I might be a wimp——"

"He's not a wimp." Kilty's voice came from behind, and Nairne and Strome turned around. He had his sleeping bag pulled around him, and he looked as if he hadn't slept in a month. "He was the first man to reach the top of Everest on the Carrington expedition, when he was only twenty-four."

"Everest? A *climber*?" Nairne felt her head spin.

"Mountaineer and photographer." Kilty's voice shook. "He had to give up climbing after that, because on the descent he wrecked one of his knees when he went down a crevasse to rescue Nick Carrington..."

"Strome!" Nairne turned to him in dismay. "Oh, dear heavens, you shouldn't have come up here... Your knee... The risk..."

He was looking at his son. And the expression in his eyes was one she had never seen there before. Gone was the hard bleakness she seen in the past, the bleakness she had expected to see now. In its place was a vulnerability that shook her...and, along with that vulnerability, she thought she glimpsed bewilderment. Bewilderment because Kilty had known who he was all along, and had kept it secret—or bewilderment because of disturbing and unfamiliar feelings germinating inside himself? Perhaps both.

Oh, both, I hope, Nairne prayed. Both, I hope.

But, even as she looked at him, he swiftly regained control of himself. His eyes became once more veiled, so that it was quite impossible to guess what his thoughts, his feelings were.

"It was a risk," he said brusquely, "I was prepared to take. So far, my knee is holding up. Here—" he scooped up Nairne's pants, making it plain that that line of conversation was closed "—these are dry now so put them on before you freeze. We've got a long, cold hike ahead of us."

CHAPTER TEN

NAIRNE stepped under the steaming spray of the shower and uttered an ecstatic moan as the hot water streamed over her, enveloping her chilled body in warmth. Closing her eyes blissfully, she let her mind wander...

Thank heavens they were all home safely...and thank heavens Strome's knee had stood up to the arduous descent of the mountain. Such a shock it had been to discover that he had once been a renowned climber—had been on the famous Carrington expedition, no less! She'd been only a schoolgirl then, but, still, she recalled watching news of the heroic rescue on TV, recalled how her young, idealistic heart had been romantically stirred by the event. She must have been about the age Kilty was now...

Ah, Kilty...

With a sigh Nairne drew her thoughts back to the present, and as she began applying shampoo to her hair she found herself reflecting upon the unhappy situation between Strome and his son. And no matter how she tried to tell herself that it wasn't her problem, that Strome was Kilty's father and he just couldn't shut the boy out of his life, it always came back to the same thing: she was Kilty's safety net. If Strome *did* spurn the boy, she would adopt him.

But, though doing so would fill her with joy, she knew, deep in her heart, that it wasn't what was best for Kilty. He needed a male role model. He needed a father.

If only... If only Strome could overcome the bitterness eroding him. But if it was still there after fifteen years—and stronger now because of his savage anger at Hazel for having kept her pregnancy a secret from him—she saw little hope of its ever being eradicated.

She had left Strome and Kilty in the kitchen eating lunch, steaming hot soup, along with a bacon and egg quiche Kyla had brought over on a flying visit from Redhillock.

When Strome had come downstairs, just after Kyla left, he'd been wearing jeans and a black cashmere sweater, his dark hair still damp, and roughly brushed back. He'd shaved, and his skin had looked so smooth that she'd longed to stroke his jaw, feel its hard angle beneath her fingertips.

She'd felt her heart give a funny little twist when Kilty had come into the kitchen shortly after. He was wearing his usual garb, the old Black Watch tartan kilt and a T-shirt...but, for the first time in as long as Nairne could remember, he hadn't purple-gelled his hair. He'd obviously shampooed it in the shower and then combed it back with his fingers. Instead of standing up in spikes, the hair, thick, and healthy-looking, albeit a little too long, was smooth and dark, and glossy as silk. And as she had looked at his face, so lean, so serious, and just a little self-conscious, she had realized with a pang why her heart had given that funny little twist: it was like looking at a mirror image of his father.

And not only the looks. The expression deep in the eyes too. The boy was as unhappy as the man——

"Nairne?"

She started as she heard someone call her name. Blinking, she realized that while she'd been so wrapped up in her thoughts she'd finished her shower and dried herself, and was now in her bedroom with her robe on, and her blow dryer in her hand.

There was an insistent knock on the door. "Nairne!" It was Strome.

"Yes?" Her grip on the dryer tightened.

"Are you all right?"

"Yes... I'll be another ten minutes——"

"Are you decent?"

"Yes," she said. "Why?"

"I want to talk to you."

Nairne could have sworn she detected a hint of panic in his voice. Placing the dryer on her dresser, she opened the door. "Come in." As he walked past her and moved across the room she asked, "What on earth's the matter?"

"I'm leaving."

"*Leaving*? But——"

"He idolizes me." Strome's face, she suddenly saw, was haggard. "Kilty... he began talking while we were eating. He told me he has a collection of my work—photographs I took over the years for magazines while I was still climbing. He told me..." He closed his eyes and Nairne saw him swallow hard, but when he went on his voice was tightly controlled and steady. "He told me that my work was his inspiration..."

"Oh, dear Lord—this was before he knew you... or who you were..."

"That's right. Then when he found out through the lawyer he hired that the man he admired so much was actually his father... and had, he believed, betrayed his mother, he felt as if in some way he had betrayed her too, and he was filled with guilt."

"But if he felt so guilty, why did he have the lawyer contact you? That is what happened, isn't it? That's how you found out about him, found out that you had a son?"

"No, Nairne, that's not how it happened. All Kilty wanted to know was his real father's identity. Nothing more, because he assumed all along that I knew about his existence and he also assumed I'd deserted his mother. Before he learned who I was he hated me—and after he knew who I was his feelings became totally confused. One part of him still wanted to hate me, but the other part couldn't bear to give up the image he had of his longtime hero."

"Oh, Strome, how dreadful for him."

"Mm. His lawyer—a Ken Bain in Inverness—had, on Kilty's instructions, hired an investigator, who dug into Hazel's past. He started, of course, at the period in her life when Kilty would have been conceived—and tracked down any eligible males who were in Glencraig around that time. Eventually my name got on his list, and he traced me to my London apartment. But, when he started asking questions about me in my local watering hole, the barman, an old buddy of mine, got curious. He asked a few leading questions of his own, and found out I was supposed to have fathered a child in Glencraig."

"When had Kilty started looking for you?"

"Right after Hugh died, but I didn't get wind of what was happening till about three weeks ago. I hired my own investigator to find out who'd been looking for me, he followed all the trails and they led him to Bain. I phoned Bain, but he wouldn't confirm the investigator's story. All he would tell me was that he was acting for a client——"

"And Bain, of course, would have contacted Kilty after your call."

"And that's why the boy opted out of the Outward Bound. Bain had warned him he suspected from something I'd said that I was planning to return to Glencraig."

"Which you did."

"Yes, I did, in order to verify the story. And now," his eyes darkened, "I'm going to leave. I've fulfilled the purpose of my trip——"

"No," Nairne cried, "you can't go, not yet."

Strome smiled, a sad smile, and, reaching out, caressed her cheek gently with the back of his hand. For a long moment he looked at her, his face drawn with unhappiness, and then he said, quietly, "You can't undo the past, Nairne. Not even with the best will in the world."

Nairne watched him walk to the door, and her breath was exhaled in a heavy sigh of unhappiness as he went out and closed it firmly behind him.

She leaned against the wall, staring unseeingly into space. No, she agreed, you can't undo the past...but you can learn to accept it, put it behind you, and look to the future. And if he wasn't concerned about his own future he should be concerned about Kilty's. He can't leave, she thought despairingly, he just can't. *Not without his son.* She wouldn't let him.

But what could she do?

She pushed herself from the wall and walked to the dresser. In the mirror she saw that her cheeks were flushed, her eyes almost feverishly bright. Biting her lip, she plugged in the hair dryer. She had to hurry, she decided as the high hum of the little motor whined in her ears. There was no time to waste.

Strome Galbraith was a man whose mind was made up.

She was prepared to do anything to change it.

Kilty was a wonderful boy, talented, responsible and possessing a special charm of his own. And he was already getting to Strome. Nairne felt something tighten in her chest as she remembered her mother saying to Kyla and Adam when Catriona was born, "It doesn't take long for a baby to twine its way around your heart." Kilty was no longer a baby, but he was still a child...*Strome's child.* And Nairne knew, with a certainty she couldn't have explained, that, given a chance, the boy would twine his way around his father's heart.

He had to.

She was counting on it.

"Are you going out?" Nairne ran down the last few steps of the staircase as she saw Kilty at the front door. To her surprise...and relief...he was wearing a jacket; it was a khaki army jerkin—probably an old one of Hugh's—and had seen better days, but it was warm and it would cut the wind.

"Aye," he said. "It's just two. I'll catch the rest of the afternoon at school."

"Will you be coming right home after?"

"Aye." His gray eyes clouded as he jerked his head in the direction of the upstairs rooms. "Though he'll be gone by then." In a muffled voice he added, "He said his goodbyes."

Nairne crossed the space between them quickly and put a hand on his forearm. "You don't want him to go, do you?"

Kilty's Adam's apple bobbed up and down. "I canna stop him." He averted his eyes, but not before Nairne saw them glisten. "He made me take the camera. A gift, he said."

Nairne tried to imagine the scene, and had to fight back the threatening tears. "I'm going to try to stop him," she whispered huskily. "I know he'll love you if he can only open up——"

"He'll no' love me." Kilty brushed the sleeve of his jerkin over his eyes, and, opening the door, stared out blindly at the snow-covered trees in front of the house. "He'll no' let himself. He's too filled wi' hate. The same as I was."

"Kilty——"

But it was too late. He pulled the door shut behind him and was gone.

There was no point in running after him, Nairne knew; what could she say to reassure him? But she *would* try to detain Strome . . . she didn't know how, and she didn't give much for her chances of success, but she was determined to try.

And she couldn't delay. He was probably packing his things at this very moment.

Smoothing down her Aran sweater, Nairne made for the stairs. Her heartbeats were racing, her palms damp. She had to stop him . . .

She knocked on the door, and when he opened it, before he had time to ask what she wanted, she stepped by him into the room.

"I thought you might want some help with your packing," she murmured, turning to him with a bright smile.

He didn't return her smile. "I've finished, thanks. I didn't have much to pack."

Nairne's glance fell to the suitcase lying by the dresser. It was already zipped up. He had tidied the room, and apart from the rumpled bedcovers there was nothing left to show that Strome Galbraith had ever been there. And, once he was in his sleek Mercedes and tooling along the highway on his road back to the city, there would be absolutely nothing left to show that he'd ever returned to Glencraig.

Nothing but the heartache he was going to leave behind.

"You can't wait to get out of here, can you?" The words came from her mouth, but she'd had no idea before she heard them that she was going to say them.

His eyes became shuttered. "I wouldn't put it exactly like——"

"I would." Where had that bold tone come from? she wondered. "And I'll say it again. You can't wait to get out of here...and I know the reason why."

"Really?" he said with a cool lift of one dark brow. "Perhaps you'd care to enlighten me?"

"Oh, I don't think I need to enlighten you." Nairne flicked back her hair and fixed him with a steady gaze. "But, since you seem determined to keep up your little pretense, I'll go along with it too. You can't wait to get out of here because...you're afraid."

His laugh was gentle, but it had a wary edge. "And what, may I ask, am I afraid of?"

"You're afraid to stay because..."

His eyes narrowed. "Go on."

"You're afraid to stay," she said softly, "because you're afraid of...of your own emotions. You're beginning to be tempted by the thought of getting to know your son, you're beginning to think about how you could nurture his talent, you're beginning to wonder if you'll be able to get him out of your mind if you don't leave right now, because you already feel that icy wall around your heart melting, and it terrifies you——"

"Wrong, Nairne." His voice was harsh. "It doesn't terrify me. But it does remind me... It reminds me of the fickleness of the human heart, it reminds me of the pain that love can bring. And it reminds me of my promise to myself that I would never let myself feel again——"

"But you are feeling again!" Nairne's voice was anguished. Hardly aware of what she was doing, she closed the space between them, and, taking his hands, she gripped them as she looked up at him fiercely. "You *are* feeling again! I can tell by the way you look at your son that deep inside you there's a yearning that's tearing you apart——"

With an abrupt twist of his hands he reversed their position so that he, now, was the one gripping her hands. He used them to pull her against him.

"If you can see so much," he said harshly, "with this magical vision of yours, then you must also be able to see the yearning I have to hold you in my arms, to make love to you. And you must be able to see that right at this moment it's a yearning I can no longer resist."

Ever since she'd come into the room she'd been all too aware of his sexual magnetism, but she had forced herself to ignore it; she had come here for Kilty's sake. But when his lips hungrily searched for hers, claiming them in a kiss that had her knees buckling, she found herself forgetting Kilty, forgetting everything except this dark, seductive man who was setting her senses reeling.

She should have known it was inevitable. Whatever this chemistry was that existed between them, though it lay sometimes deeper below the surface than at other times, it was there always. And it was irresistible always. So with a little moan, deep in her throat, she accepted it, leaning weakly into him. And as she slid her arms around his neck he put his arms around her waist and pulled her even closer. As if they had been made for each other, their bodies fitted, she acknowledged in some distant part of her brain—the last functioning part of her brain, before it closed down completely and left her senses in charge. And her senses, she realized with something akin to panic, were totally irresponsible.

They urged her to stand on her tiptoe and, with a hunger that equaled his own, give herself to his kiss. They urged her to part her lips, so that his sweetly persuasive tongue could find its way to the secret recesses of her mouth. They urged her to yield when his knee thrust demandingly between her thighs. They urged her to wind her fingers through his thick dark hair and pull his head even closer, so that they were as close as if they were one.

Yes, her senses did urge her on recklessly, and yes, she did give in to their wild and wanton urgings. She didn't resist when she felt hard, warm fingers pull her Aran sweater up over her breasts; she didn't resist when she felt his thumbs tease the tips of her breasts, which rose eagerly to greet them...

"You're a witch," he murmured into her auburn hair, "a veritable Highland witch. You've cast a spell over me, and the Lord only knows how I'm going to escape——"

"Do you want to escape?" Nairne breathed out the question as she pressed against him.

He framed his face with her hands and she looked into eyes that were glazed with passion. "At this moment the last thing I want to do is escape," he murmured. He slid his hands down over her waist and behind her, cupping her buttocks. "What I want to do is——"

"Oh, I can tell very well what you want to do!" Nairne retorted weakly as he guided her back toward the bed. "You want to——"

"Make love to you." His mouth closed off her words, and he lowered her gently onto the duvet.

She might have managed to resist him had his male scent not been so irresistible to her. He was still wearing his City Man, and she was still aware that some other woman had given it to him; but that scent was superficial. Below it, and superceding it, was his own masculine scent. Musky, earthy, quintessentially male, and fashioned by nature to seek out the most secret nerve endings of the mate he desired ...

Essence of Galbraith.

There was no resisting it.

And, even if she'd wanted to, she didn't have a chance ...

Nairne felt a voluptuous languor creep over her body as she lay back on the bed. He lay over her, supported by his hands. Eyes glazed, cheeks a little flushed, there was no mistaking his desire. And she knew at that moment, with a woman's intuition, that, whatever she asked of him, he would be powerless to resist.

"You'll stay," she whispered, "just till tomorrow? Spend some time with Kilty?"

His eyes became hooded. "You want me to?"

She nodded. "I want you to."

As she said the words she wasn't sure if she said them because of Kilty ... or because of herself. She wanted him to stay for Kilty's sake, of course ... but did she want him to stay because she didn't want him to go?

"Then I'll stay," he said softly.

"You promise?"

"I promise." With gentle fingers he spread her long auburn hair over the pillow and, with his breath warm on her skin, planted tantalizing little kisses on her parted lips, as if feeding her with exquisite morsels of manna. Manna for which she immediately developed an insatiable hunger. More, she urged silently, greedily; more ...

"But now," he skimmed his mouth away from hers, over the delicate curve of her jaw toward her ear, immediately, incredibly focusing on an achingly sensitive

spot that seemed to be linked by a sensual thread of ecstasy to every other erotic point in her body, "let's forget
about tomorrow..."

Her heated flesh hummed with expectation as she felt
his hand at her waist, sliding under the hem of her
sweater. Possessively he ran his slightly callused palm
over her naked midriff, up and down, up and down, as
if savoring the satiny texture of her skin...and with each
movement sliding closer and closer to the swell of her
breast. She felt her nipple tug against the tight lace of
her bra, felt another—even more intense—response
quivering deep inside her...

With a little moan she twisted sideways, protesting
against the almost painful sensations thrilling through
her, sensations of longing that were driving her mind-
lessly toward a sweet and unknown destiny...a destiny
shimmering with the colors of a rainbow...

"Shy, my sweet?" Strome murmured as he rested his
weight on the bed and, catching her left hand in his,
twined his fingers through hers. "Look at me." Softly
given though the order was, it was compelling.

After a long, tension-filled moment Nairne finally
lifted her eyelids...eyelids that seemed as heavy as if
she was in a stupor. She wanted to look at him, but found
herself instead dropping her gaze to their two hands.
Male and female. Just the sight of their hands twined
together sent another thrill of sensation swooning over
her. His so strong and masterful, with dark hair curling
over his tanned skin—hers so feminine and yielding, with
freckles peppering her ivory skin...and something
glinting on one finger in the buttery afternoon sunlight
slanting through the window——

Her ring. Her wedding ring. The ring Rory had placed
so devotedly on her finger after they had pronounced
their wedding vows.

She closed her eyes as pain shafted through her.
Pain...and guilt.

It was no use.

Despair screamed in her ears as she realized she couldn't go through with it...this intimacy she had let herself become involved in. The past was still too much with her. Her thoughts...she couldn't control her thoughts. For a short time she and Strome had been alone in the room, but now there was someone else there with them.

"I'm sorry," she whispered, sliding her fingers from his and laying her arm across her eyes as she felt tears pricking there. "I can't do this—I feel as if..."

"As if you're betraying Rory."

There was a deep, heavy weariness in his voice. Self-derision. Bleakness. Acceptance. She felt her heart cry out, but she couldn't change the way she felt.

"I feel," her whispered words were threaded with anguish, regret, pain, "as if he's..."

She became aware of the shifting of the mattress under her back, and realized he was getting up. A moment later she sensed that he was standing by the bed, looking down at her, and then she felt his fingers curl around her wrist. As he gently lifted her arm from across her eyes she opened them, and looked up.

"It's all right, Nairne." His eyes were still dark with passion, but his voice was...kind, reassuring...as if he were talking to a child. "I understand how you feel. I would never ask you to do anything you didn't want to do. Lovemaking, real lovemaking, can never be one-sided—the woman has to want it as much as the man..."

I do want you, something inside Nairne pleaded, I do want you, but I need time.

She had no right to ask this man for time; and if she did, why would he give her it? There must be many women in his life who would eagerly jump at the chance of making love with him—women who didn't need time...

She realized he was again holding her hand, and she let him pull her up beside him. Powerless to draw away, she looked up at him, her breath paralyzed in her throat.

"If you were any other woman," he said softly, "I'd have suspected you of being a tease. I'd have suspected that you used your feminine wiles to seduce me into making a promise—a promise that I would stay. But you——" he wove his fingers through the auburn curls tumbling over her forehead and swept them back '—you, with your transparently honest violet eyes, are capable of no such deceit."

Had she used her so-called feminine wiles to persuade him to stay? Confusion twisted inside Nairne. Certainly she'd had no intention of deceiving him, of tricking him... but perhaps she had. Who was she deceiving, she wondered despairingly... Strome—or herself? Yes, she wanted him to stay, to give Kilty a chance to win him over, but if she was to be completely honest she had to admit that she had felt an intense churning of her emotions when he'd made his promise to stay. She had to be honest with him...

But, even as she opened her mouth to try to set the record straight, his fingertip stroked over her lips.

"Don't," he said simply. "You don't have to explain yourself to me. I understand." Brushing a kiss over her crown, he stood back and let her go.

It seemed like an eternity that she just looked at him, aching for him, yearning for him... but unable to take the step that would bring her into his arms again. Finally, with a choking feeling in her throat, she stumbled past him and crossed the room to the door. He didn't try to stop her... and she hadn't expected him to.

If he understood her, Nairne thought miserably as she crossed the landing and went downstairs, it was more than she did. She was completely bewildered by the conflicting emotions raging inside herself. She wanted him with an urgency that terrified her... yet her feelings of guilt were even stronger than her desire.

Would those feelings of guilt ever disappear? Would she one day be able to open herself up completely to another man, let him into her life, into her bed, without Rory and his memory coming between them?

She bent to pat Shadow as he came up the stairs to meet her. "Life's become such a muddle, old friend," she whispered. "Will it clear, once our B and B leaves again?"

Shadow wagged his tail joyfully, as if he thought, Yes, it would certainly clear when Strome had gone.

Nairne sighed. She wished she could be only half as sure...

CHAPTER ELEVEN

"GOOD NIGHT, Nairne. I'm off to bed."

As Kilty's voice came from the open doorway behind her Nairne twisted around in her armchair by the living-room fire. "You've finished setting up the darkroom?"

"Aye. Thanks for letting me use the space."

"Oh, that little garden room next to the kitchen has been sitting empty for years . . . and, having a sink, it will suit your purpose nicely. The equipment and supplies Strome bought for you in Inverness—you're pleased with them?"

"How could I not be? Everything's the very best." Kilty attempted to inject a jaunty note into his voice, but it sounded false in Nairne's ears. When he'd come home from school and found his father still at Bruach she'd seen the instant spark of joy in his gray eyes . . . but Strome had quickly extinguished that spark by saying in a deliberately casual tone that he'd just decided to leave next day; it made more sense, he explained, to set off early while the roads were still quiet. He had, however, told Kilty he wanted to take him to Inverness on a shopping trip, and the two of them had set off ten minutes later. They had eaten out and arrived back at Bruach at nine-thirty, when they'd immediately started setting up a darkroom for Kilty. Wanting to be with them, but knowing she should leave them on their own, Nairne had stayed in the living room. But she *had* gone to the kitchen to make a cup of tea around ten, and she couldn't help overhearing their voices as she had passed the open doorway of the garden room—Kilty asking questions, a gruffness in his tone that was designed to hide his emotions, and Strome's deeper voice answering the questions with an ease that came from his vast knowledge of photography. The rapport between the two was unmistakable, a rapport strengthened by their shared interest. Nairne had felt her heart ache as she listened to the harmony of the voices—felt it ache for Kilty, who so desperately wanted to give his love...and felt it ache even more for Strome, who was fighting such an anguished struggle against taking it.

"Yes, you're right, Strome would buy only the best." Nairne put her book down and got up. "Where is he?"

"He said he was going upstairs."

"Oh." He'd gone to bed. Nairne felt a great welling of disappointment. All the time he'd been with Kilty— when they'd been away in Inverness, and again when they'd been busy in the garden room—she'd tried to read *Desire's Dark Dawn*, but her thoughts had kept turning to Strome. She'd found herself staring into the fire, thinking about him, thinking about the way she yearned for him. And now she realized she'd been all wound up, waiting for Kilty to go to bed, wondering what might happen between herself and——

"I'm off, then, Nairne."

Nairne blinked. "Oh..." Picking up her empty cup and saucer, she walked across the room. She put one arm around Kilty's shoulder and gave him a hug. "Good night. I'll see you in the morning."

A few moments later, rinsing her dishes in the kitchen, she found herself wondering what the new darkroom looked like. No harm in peeking in, she decided...

The door was closed, but as she opened it she felt her heart give a violent lurch. Strome hadn't gone upstairs after all; he was over by the sink, reaching above his head, obviously making some adjustment to the blind on the window.

He turned, his expression questioning. "Oh, it's you," he said evenly. "I thought Kilty had forgotten something."

Nairne stared at him, feeling as if she were drowning. As he stretched up, continuing his task, his fine cotton shirt was stretched over his shoulders and back, delineating his hard muscles, his perfectly proportioned shape. His jacket and tie were slung over the back of a chair beside him, and he'd rolled up his shirtsleeves to just below his elbow, revealing his strong forearms covered with black, springy hair. Masculinity emanated from every line of his body, from the shadowed angle of his jaw and the taut curve of his buttocks under his gray pants to the powerful thrust of his thighs as he braced himself against the sink.

Why was it, she wondered dazedly, that when she was in a room with him her surroundings faded away, and all she was conscious of was him? And his effect on her? This faint, dizzy feeling...

"There," he said, and brushed his hands together, "that should do it. Kilty's all set up again."

Nairne tried not to look at his hands, hands that had touched her body so intimately. "Tell me," she said in an effort to distract her straying thoughts, "why did you give up your own photography, since you had so much talent? You were very angry when I told you Kilty had given up his—I seem to recall your saying that, when God gave someone a talent, that person had a duty to——"

"I didn't give up my career by choice, Nairne."

"Well, no," she said, walking across the room and taking up a stance as far from him as possible, "I can understand that you wouldn't be able to climb Everest with a wonky knee, but the photography——"

"My photography and my climbing were inextricably intertwined. First there was the challenge presented by the mountain, and then there was the challenge of depicting the relationship between man and mountain through the eyes of the camera. Yes, you're right—when I wrecked my knee my mountaineering days were over." He shrugged, and there was a self-derisive edge to his tone as he went on, "But, in the rock slide that occurred when I was climbing down the crevasse to get Nick, I also suffered head injuries...and the blow irreparably damaged the optic nerve in my right eye. I can't see a damned thing with it."

Nairne couldn't hide her shock. Stunned, she stared at him. "But..." Whatever she had been going to say trailed away awkwardly.

"But the eye looks fine?" He laughed, an easy laugh. "Oh, Nairne, don't be afraid of saying the wrong thing— I'm not sensitive about having the use of only one eye. Granted, it took me a while to accept the fact that my climbing days were over, and the photography too, but I was lucky to be alive, and when I got back on my feet again I looked around for something else to do. I'd played with the idea of building mountaineering lodges when I eventually had to retire from climbing—so when that day came earlier than I'd anticipated I just moved my plans forward. I found a backer, and built the first Crest Mountain Lodge. It was a success...and from that time on I've never looked back."

"Isn't it strange," Nairne said quietly, "that your son inherited not only your love of climbing, but also your talent for photography?"

She saw a nerve flicker in his cheek. "Yes," he said tersely, "it is." He scraped the back of one hand over his jaw. "I can foresee that one day he'll make a good living at it."

"Strome...did you ever find out why he took your wallet that first morning?"

"He told me tonight. He just wanted to look at my ID, wanted to verify that I was really Strome Somerled Galbraith...really his father." His laughter had a hollow sound. "It seems he's also inherited some of my skepticism."

He turned away, as if to let Nairne know he didn't want to talk about his son. "The moon's quite bright tonight," he said, his voice a little rough. "This is a good time to check that there are no chinks of light getting in."

Before Nairne realized what he was going to do he had crossed to the door, and shut it, and clicked off the light.

All of sudden, they were plunged into a darkness that to Nairne was as suffocating as if she'd been dropped into a vat of black cotton wool. Feeling as if she couldn't breathe, she fumbled her way toward the door, but before she could reach it she found herself up against a wall of hard-muscled flesh.

"Whoa..." Strome grasped her around the ribs. "Watch out—you could get hurt walking around in the dark."

Because of the blackness surrounding them it felt to Nairne as if she had stepped into another world, a world that was completely detached from reality. All that existed for her was Strome. There was nothing in the room but the echo of his voice in her ears, rich and sweet as dark honey; the pressure of his hands on her ribs, firm and strong; and the invisible aura that enmeshed her in its spell—his body heat, his sexual magnetism, his maleness.

She could see nothing, but could feel shock zinging through every nerve in her body, as if by touching her he had completed an electrical circuit, enabling a supercharged current to pulse breathtakingly between them.

She cleared her throat. "It's going to be a perfect darkroom..." She had hoped that if she spoke, and spoke lightly, it would defuse the sizzling tension, but the words came out not lightly, as she'd meant them to, but in a trembling, high-pitched rush.

"Oh, yes," the honeyed voice now held a slightly wary note, "it's a marvelous darkroom. Kilty couldn't have a better place for..."

Whatever he had been going to say was lost in the moan that came from Nairne's throat, the moan that was an involuntary protest as she felt him draw his hands from her ribs, the moan that of its own volition changed before she could control it into a little mew of wanting...

Wanting over which she had no control, for all of a sudden it was more than a wanting...it was a hunger, a wild, singing hunger, and, as the hunger took over, her ears closed to the voices in her mind that were crying out in alarm.

Somehow, despite the pitch-dark, she found his upper arms with her searching fingertips, and quickly she grasped them, feeling his warm flesh through the fine cotton, feeling the hard, rippling muscles she'd been watching just a few moments before. In a swift movement she followed the line of his shoulders with her palms, and then she had her hands clasped around his neck, and she was on tiptoe, pulling his head down to hers. And a second after she heard his startled "What the——?" she unerringly found his lips with her own, and closed off his words with a kiss that held all the pent-up longing she felt for him.

Strome's body went rigid. The hands that had been resting on her hips tightened, the body that had been close to hers pulled back, the muscles at his nape where her fingers were twined knotted.

He twisted his mouth away. "Don't do this, Nairne," he said roughly. "You mustn't——"

Nairne arched her body against his, and Strome's words of protest dragged into a groan. She slipped her fingers into his hair, twisting the tips through the thick, dark strands, glorying in the silky texture, and felt her heartbeats lurch forward erratically as she felt his body responding to the feminine, yielding movements of her own.

A great sigh shuddered through her as the hands at her midriff gripped her savagely, and the lips that had been reluctant to accept her kisses now hungrily responded to her insistent demands. And all at once the body that had been rigid against hers became her cradle, a cradle in which her female curves were possessively nestled. A cradle of strong arms, muscled chest, flat stomach, hard thighs...

Every outline, every ridge was impressed against her, and she felt her knees weaken as she became joltingly aware of just how aroused he was. A wild excitement rushed through her as she realized the power she had over him, the effect her aggressive actions had had on him. But it wasn't so surprising, considering what was happening to her own body; it seemed to be dissolving into a hot liquid stream; she seemed to be melting into him, as if they had become one.

With a sigh she gave herself up to the blissful sensation, the flowing, mindless sensation, closing her eyes, relaxing her lips. And, as her lips parted, his tongue, warm and taut, arrogant, now taking charge, sought hers. And with each bold thrust from him, each answering provocative parry from her, the heat joining them grew more and more intense.

She knew that if he hadn't been cradling her in his arms she would have keeled over helplessly; she felt as tipsy as if she'd drunk a bottle of champagne and the bubbles were sparkling in her bloodstream and effervescing in her brain. A brain that had stopped functioning, as it always did when she was in his arms.

"You're like a drug. I keep wanting and wanting you." His words were breathed against her lips, his fingers searching her hair for the clasps that confined her auburn curls. "There," he said on a groan, and she heard a tiny clatter in the dark as he tossed the clasps down somewhere, "that's better."

Nairne could feel his hand in her hair, feel him running the glossy strands through his fingertips, over and over, as if he couldn't get enough of the sensuous feel of it. She didn't protest when his hand moved down over her nape, caressing her for a moment before following the curve of her shoulder...and then he was sliding open the buttons of her silk blouse. In a moment she felt it slipping down over her shoulders, felt her hair brushing her naked skin. His fingertips tickled her spine as he opened the clasp of her bra; his breath was a harsh sigh as the clasp came undone, and her full breasts spilled out.

"Oh, Nairne..." The words trembled from him as if it was only with the greatest effort that he could speak. His fingers shook as he stroked them over her skin, over her midriff, up the rounded swell of her breasts, cupping them for a long moment, before with a sigh he brushed the pads of his thumbs over the softly peaked nipples.

Nairne felt a ripple of sensation shiver to her core on a silken thread of ecstasy, arousing an exquisite quivering she'd never experienced before. But even as she moaned, even as she writhed, wanting more of this silvery nameless delight, she heard him groan again, this time a painful sound, a sound that seemed to come from somewhere deep and dark inside him.

She froze as he drew his lips from hers and pulled her head against his chest. "Dear heaven," his voice was anguished. "I can't do this... You shouldn't have... I shouldn't have... It's all wrong..."

For a moment Nairne didn't understand what he was saying. Her breasts had swollen at his touch, her body was being consumed by a flooding desire, she was helpless in his hands... and he was saying...

"Why not?" she whispered. She heard the dismay, the frustration, the anguish in her own voice, but she was beyond caring. She wanted this man, with a raw desire that left no room for modesty or shyness. "What...?"

"It's wrong..." His voice was muffled against her hair. "Lord knows I want you... and you want me too. But I won't take you, because I know how you'll feel afterward. You'll be torn with guilt... and you'll hate me. Yes, you can give me your body... but you're the kind of woman who should never make love unless she can give her heart too. And your heart isn't yours to give. It still belongs to Rory."

Rory!

Nairne felt cold reality hit her, harshly, jarringly, as if she had been up in the heavens in a dream, and on wakening had careered down to earth without a parachute. Winded, stunned, she forced herself to face a fact that shook her to the very depths of her being—from the time that Kilty and Strome had left for Inverness till this very moment *she had never not even once thought of Rory*.

What did it mean? What could it mean...?

There was, of course, only one thing that it could mean: her heart wanted to live again, her heart was reaching out. But it not only wanted to live again...

It also wanted to love again.

And the process had already begun.

Yes, it was soon, far too soon. She had thought, after Rory died, that it would never happen. But it had. And the wonder of it was almost more than she could bear.

"Strome..." She cupped his head in her hands and raised it so that his face was close to her own, though she couldn't see it. She was sure his eyes were glistening with tears, as were her own. "My heart is healing, I can feel it. I would never have believed it would happen, but it has, and I thank God for it. It's drawn to you, and I know that, given time, I could love you, if you would let me. What I feel for you isn't just desire——"

He stroked her hair, brushing it back from her brow. "If it were possible for me to love anyone, sweet Nairne, it would be you, and I would give you all the time in the world. I would give you forever. But——" He reached behind her and with a sigh switched on the light.

He took her hands from his face, and, clasping her slender fingers tightly, held their twined hands between them... separating them.

"You deserve more than I can give," he said in a husky voice. "When a man and a woman love they should settle for nothing less than a heart that is whole. And a whole heart."

He was talking like a man whose own heart had been irrevocably broken.

Nairne forgot about her own pain, her own humiliation at being rejected, as she let his anguish wash over her, overwhelming her with its poignancy. It was too much; she couldn't stand it a minute longer.

"I'm going up now," she said raggedly. Slipping her fingers from his, she fumblingly redid the buttons of her blouse. "You're...still planning to leave in the morning?"

"Nairne, I have to go. To stay would be..." He spread his hands out before him in a beseeching gesture, as if begging her to see how he felt. "I've explained everything to the boy. He understands."

"*He needs you*, Strome."

She saw him flinch, as if she had hit him, saw his shoulders slump, as if the life was draining out of him.

"I need you too," she whispered through her tears.

He turned away.

She closed her eyes for a moment, as if by shutting out the sight of him she could shut out his torment...and her own.

Then she raised her heavy lids again and said, "What time are you leaving?"

"I'd like to get on the road by six."

"I'll see you in the morning. I'll make breakfast for you before you go."

She didn't wait for him to reply. She knew she had to get out of the room and close the door behind her, before she gave in to the aching sobs that were desperately struggling to be set free.

CHAPTER TWELVE

"Has he gone?"

Nairne brushed the perspiration from her brow as she heard Kilty's voice coming from the kitchen doorway behind her. Dropping the scrubbing brush into the bucket of hot soapy water, she sat back on her heels and, turning around, looked up at him. The look on his face twisted her heart.

She got up, and wiped her hands on the seat of her jeans. "Yes," she said quietly. "He's gone."

Kilty's Adam's apple bobbed up and down, and he turned away, looking out of the window. "I was hoping..." His voice was tight with emotion.

"Yes..." Nairne moved over and stood beside him. She put an arm around his shoulders. "Yes," she murmured, tightening her grip, "I know. I was hoping too."

"You...liked him, didn't you?"

She didn't try to hide her feelings. "More than that, Kilty, so very much more. And I wanted him to stay, just as you did. But Hazel hurt him too much. Don't hate him——"

He swiveled around, and his cheeks were wet with tears. "I dinna hate him, Nairne. What I dinna understand is how Mam could have hurt him like that. It wasna her way."

Nairne felt a cold shiver skim down her spine. "No," she whispered, "it wasn't Hazel's way. But we'll never know what was going on in her mind...or her heart...at that time." For a long moment they stood together, neither saying anything, their sorrow like a bond between them. Finally, with a heavy sigh, Nairne made to turn away, but as she did her attention was caught by the sealed white envelope lying on the windowsill.

170

"Oh..." She stepped over and picked it up. "I almost forgot... This is for you. Strome left it..."

"For me?" Kilty frowned as he took it, confusion on his lean features. "What's inside, Nairne?"

She shook her head. "I've no idea. Probably a letter." And if it was then he should probably be on his own to read it, she decided. He looked close to breaking down...and he wouldn't want her to see that. "Why don't you go through to the living room and open it? I'll just finish this floor. If you need me, give me a shout."

She had told the truth when she'd said she didn't know what was in the envelope. All she knew was that it wasn't money. Before he left, Strome had told her he'd opened an account in the Glencraig savings bank for his son, and had asked her to tell Kilty to go in there as soon as possible and sign the appropriate forms. He had also given Nairne his London address, and told her she should begin adoption proceedings right away, and he would cooperate fully. His face when he'd been speaking to her, as they had stood by the Mercedes together, had been——

No! She didn't want to remember the look in his eyes. Cold, distant, shuttered, as if he was shutting out not only her, but also life itself... She couldn't bear it.

"*Nairne!*"

She swiveled around as she heard Kilty's harsh shout; throat tight with tears, she swallowed hard as she heard his running steps in the hall. Lips parted, she gazed in bewilderment at him as he bounded into the room waving a letter wildly above his head. He'd obviously forgotten the floor was wet, as he slipped, but, righting himself with a gleeful laugh, he skated over to her on his stockinged feet.

Nairne wondered if he'd gone mad. Tears were rolling down his cheeks...but his eyes were bright with joy.

"It's in here!" He put his arms around her and, with surprising strength, lifted her off her feet and, whooping at the pitch of his voice, whirled her a round twice before dropping her again. "It's in here! Oh, Nairne..." He couldn't go on—tears were choking him—and, shaking his head, he held out the letter to her.

Tentatively Nairne took it. A frowning glance told her it was a letter... a letter to Strome...

A letter from Hazel.

"Oh, Kilty," her voice was disbelieving, "is this——?"

"Yes, it's the letter Mam wrote..."

"The letter she wrote to Strome after he went back to London, the letter he talked about." Nairne felt her stomach cramp, and she pressed one hand flat against it in a vain effort to stop the feeling of nausea rising inside her. "But this is private, Kilty. I shouldn't be reading——"

"Read it."

She could see that he had recovered from his burst of hysteria. His face was pale, his voice was shaking. He pointed at the letter in her hand. "Read it, Nairne, and you'll understand."

She could only do as she was bid. Though his voice had been tremulous, it had held a steely thread of resolve. He was giving her no choice.

The paper shook as she started to read the words on the page. It was a short letter, and written in Hazel's familiar rounded hand. It was just as Strome had told them; the letter was a typical "Dear John" letter, announcing that their affair was over, she was in love with someone else. She was in love with Hugh... and always had been...

I knew it as soon as I saw him striding up the road when he came back from the fishing. I'm sorry, Strome. I guess I was lonely, and you came on the scene at a time...

"Don't you see Nairne?"

Nairne stared wide-eyed at Kilty as he snatched the letter back from her. "'I knew it as soon as I saw him striding up the road——'"

"Ooh." Nairne sucked in her breath as if someone had punched her in the stomach. "Ooh..." Her legs started to give way under her, and, stumbling back, she fumbled for a chair and sank down on it.

Kilty whooped again and threw the letter in the air. It floated down and landed in Nairne's bucket, settling on top of the soapy water.

"What are we going to do, Nairne? What are we going to do?"

"Whew..." Nairne shook her head, wondering if it really was spinning around and around as it felt it was. "I just can't believe it... But we should have known... We should have guessed...it was something like this. Your Mam never would have hurt anyone...unless she had to..."

"Unless by not hurting them...she would have hurt someone else even more." Kilty closed his eyes for a moment. "Oh, Nairne. What a sacrifice she made."

"Yes," Nairne whispered, "what a sacrifice. And the one who was hurt the most...was Strome."

"He put a note in the envelope saying he had always carried this letter around, had somehow never been able to bring himself to throw it out. He wanted me to have it—it would be proof, he said, that he wasn't lying about what happened between him and Mam."

"He couldn't have dreamed that the letter would do more than that." Nairne drew in a deep breath. "Kilty, we have to...make things right."

"I know... But how?"

She got up, shakily. Taking Kilty by the hand, she led him across to her desk in the windowed alcove. "Sit down." She pulled out the chair and he plonked himself down on it and looked up at her. "It's going to be up to you," she said, giving his shoulder an encouraging squeeze. "You must write him a letter explaining everything, and you must send it by courier. It should be in London almost before he is!" She pushed a pad of her rough cream-colored writing paper in front of him, and a matching envelope with her gold monogram on it, and handed him a pen.

"Write and tell him what's in your heart, and then we shall just have to wait. I know it won't be for long."

How wrong she had been.

And how foolish.

She had sat up all night, expecting any minute to hear the phone, to hear Strome's voice, telling her he'd received the letter, and that he was coming back right away. Kilty had stayed up with her till around midnight, but eventually, with the excited, anticipatory sparkle gone from his eyes, he had hitched up his kilt wearily and gone to bed.

Next day, drawn and pale, Nairne chastised herself for her impatience—and tried to bolster Kilty's confidence before he left for school. "Your father will phone today, for sure," she said in as reassuring voice as she could muster...

But he didn't.

And he didn't phone the next day, or the next, or the day after.

"He doesna care." Kilty had withdrawn into himself. Nairne could only guess at how rejected he must feel. "He's no' going to change. It's too late."

Was he right?

By the end of the second week Nairne felt the last of her own hopes fading; Strome Galbraith had been only a ship that had passed in the night. They would never see him again; he had come north to fulfill his financial obligations to his son, and, that done, he had shut him...and Nairne...out of his mind.

How she wished she could shut him out as easily from hers.

The wind was unseasonably warm on the Sunday morning the boys were due back from the Outward Bound. Nairne, dressed in a Fair Isle sweater and light blue jeans, stood on the front doorstep for a few moments as she came out of the house to see if there was any sign of the bus. Glancing at her watch, she saw that it should be arriving any minute, and she began walking down the drive toward the gate.

The snowdrops were past, she noticed sadly. Brown, limp, withered, they hung on listless stems, knowing that their place was going to be taken soon by the daffodils and tulips that were already pushing their way up through the damp earth.

She lifted her face to the spring sun, soaking up its reluctant warmth. Way in the distance she heard the sound of a plane—no, not a plane, she realized as she shaded her eyes from the sun and searched the skies, a helicopter. Probably from the naval base——

The loud tooting of a horn drew her attention back to the road. There, chugging around the corner of the drive, was the small yellow bus.

Her boys were back.

So much had happened while they were away, she reflected with a sigh, even as she raised a hand and sketched a cheery wave in the direction of the ancient vehicle. But it was all in the past now. She must look to the future.

A moment later she was surrounded by a flurry of deep-voiced teenagers with weather-beaten faces and shaggy hair and cheeky grins. Backpacks and cases littered the drive, along with pieces of driftwood and a clutter of odds and ends.

"Looks as if you all had a good time," she said with a welcoming smile.

A chorus of "Yeah! Yeah!", "Smashing!", and "Bloody hard work, Nairne!" met her ears over the sound of the bus's idling engine.

She grinned. "Well, I'm sure you're all starving after that long bus ride——"

She was interrupted by a groan from Archie, a lanky six footer. "We havena eaten since six this morning!"

"I've set the table in the kitchen for you. You'll find sausages and bacon and scrambled eggs in the oven, milk and orange juice in the fridge—help yourselves, and I'll——"

They were gone before she'd finished speaking, jostling each other playfully as they bounded away toward the front door.

Nairne shook hands with their leader. "Mr. Webster, thanks for bringing them all home safely."

"We had a grand trip, Nairne. One of the best. Too bad about young Kilty, though. How is he?"

"Oh—er—he's fine now."

"I didn't want to send him back on his own, but there was no option but to put him on a bus. And I sensed that there was something eating at the laddie—that his problems weren't so much physical as——"

"You did the right thing." Nairne didn't want to get into discussing Kilty with Dan Webster; his problems were private. "Now, I won't keep you, Dan—I'm sure your wife's anxious to have you home again."

"Och, Bess likes my annual jaunt to the west coast—gives her a chance to do her spring-cleaning without me underfoot!" He jumped back into the cab of the bus, and with a "Cheerio, Nairne!" chugged away along the drive.

Nairne looked at her watch again. Kilty had taken Shadow and his Nikon and gone for a walk, and had said he'd go to the cemetery on his way home. She would just check on the boys, and then she'd put on her jacket and go along to the cemetery herself, meet him there——

Now that the sounds of the bus had faded away she realized she could once more hear the helicopter she'd heard earlier. It sounded very much closer. Frowning, she raised her gaze to the sky...

And felt her heart give a great lurch.

For heaven's sake, it looked as if the chopper was going to land in the field next door to Bruach, at Craigend. Her pulse fluttered as alarm rippled through her. Was something wrong? The engine sounded even enough, but there could be other problems. Perhaps the pilot had taken ill.

Without stopping to think, Nairne ran across to the fence dividing the two properties, and, ducking between the strands of wire, straightened on the other side and sped across the grass as if she had wings on her shoes. When she was still half a field away from the helicopter it had set itself down.

And, by the time she was thirty feet from it, the door had slid open, and someone was dropping out onto the ground. A man. A man in a black leather jacket, and black cords. A man who was tall, dark, devastatingly attractive...

And devastatingly familiar.

Nairne stopped as suddenly as if she'd run into a brick wall. He'd come back. After all, he had come back. Elation unfolded inside her chest like the petals of a wonderful multicolored blossom, and all at once everything around her had a soft pink tinge.

"Strome..." The word came out in a whisper.

She couldn't have moved if her life had depended on it, but it didn't matter. He came all the way. And, even as she pinched herself to see if it was really happening, he picked her up and whirled her around till her head was spinning. Like father, like son, she thought with a touch of hysteria; both, it seemed, were fond of whirling people off their feet when they were happy.

And Strome *was* happy. His face was open as he set her down and pulled her hard against him—his features relaxed, his eyes warm and full of love.

"I nearly made the biggest mistake of my life," he said huskily, burying his face in her hair. "I almost didn't see that I'd fallen in love with you, that I need you, I can't live without you. Am I too late?" The eyes that looked into hers saw the answer, and the lips that met hers sealed a bargain that had no need to be put into words.

"Oh, Strome," she managed to say finally, "I was praying you'd come back when Kilty sent——"

"Kilty." Strome brushed back the strands of auburn hair that were being gusted around her cheeks as the helicopter lifted into the air again. "Where is he?"

"He's gone to the cemetery," she said softly. "He'll be so thrilled to see you. Why don't you go and meet him there——?"

"And you, my love?"

"I'll wait."

His mouth claimed hers again in a kiss that stole her very soul. She closed her eyes, and gave herself in to the perfection of it——

Piercing whistles and raucous laughter broke into the moment of ecstasy, and with a gasp Nairne twisted her head around and saw her boys standing gleefully at the fence.

"Right on, Nairne!" they shouted as one.

Strome didn't release his possessive grip. "These heathens are yours?" Laughter trembled in his voice. "I have to take them on, too, if I take you?"

"I'm afraid so." She stood on tiptoe and kissed him. "Too much for you?" she challenged.

"I'll keep them so busy that they won't know what's hit them," he retorted. "I've arranged for work to start here, at Craigend, within the week. I'm going to build that mountaineering lodge I planned on years ago...and there'll be jobs for everybody, for as long as they want to work.''

"Oh, Strome..." Nairne breathed a sigh of pure contentment. "So you'll be around for a while?"

"I'll be around forever," he protested. "You can count on it."

The boys had all gone home, and Nairne was alone in the kitchen, cleaning up. After putting the last plate into the dishwasher she poured cold water into the coffee maker, and plugged it in. But her mind wasn't on what she was doing; it was at the other end of Glencraig, trying to imagine the scene at the cemetery—Strome and Kilty, standing together at Hazel's grave, all the bitter misunderstandings over.

She paused, and stared unseeingly out of the window. If only...

With a frustrated exclamation she tried to close her mind to the "if only," but it wouldn't be shut out. She sighed, and made herself face up to her innermost thoughts. Things would have been perfect, she admitted with harsh honesty, if Strome had come to her with a heart full of love—and if he had come to his son with a heart full of love—*before*, not after, he had found out the truth about Hazel. If only he'd struggled with himself after returning to London, she thought wistfully, struggled to overcome his bitterness and succeeded ... and discovered in the process that putting the past behind him was necessary in order for him to be happy once again. Then he really would have been her shining silver knight, someone who had faced up to fortune's "slings and arrows' and dealt with them courageously, despite the wounds suffered on the way——

Nairne shrugged. So he wasn't perfectly shiny, this man of hers. Surely she could live with a little tarnish——

She jerked herself back to the present as she heard the front door open. Drying her hands on her jeans, she turned, and as Strome came into the kitchen she felt her heart melt with love for him. He held out his arms and she ran into them. "Where's Kilty?" she whispered against his chest.

"He went down the glen to take some pictures." Strome planted a kiss on her crown. "He said to give you this."

Nairne stared blankly at the envelope he held out to her, an envelope with her distinctive gold monogram in one corner. It was addressed to Strome, in Kilty's handwriting. It couldn't be...surely it couldn't be...the letter she'd told him to write to Strome, revealing the truth about Hazel's motivation for marrying Hugh? But the envelope was still sealed. Yet it *had* to be that letter... "I don't understand," she said faintly.

"He said you wouldn't. I sure as hell don't!" He raked a bewildered hand through his dark hair. "He said— now let me get this right—'Tell Nairne I never sent it. I wanted him to want us badly enough to come for us.'"

Tears welled in Nairne's eyes as she took the envelope from him. "Oh," she said chokingly, "what a wise boy he is. Far wiser than I——"

"It's addressed to me." Strome's voice was taut. "May I read it?"

Yes, of course she was going to let him read it. And she could understand why Kilty had wanted *her* to give Strome the letter; the boy knew the truth would rip his father apart and he couldn't bear to see it.

"Yes," she said, her voice husky with tears. She pulled out a chair. "Sit here," she tried to keep her voice light, but didn't succeed, "and if you'll excuse me for a moment I'll go and put some logs on the living room fire." She poured him a mug of coffee and set it at his elbow. "There you are," she said. "There's more in the pot if you want it. I'll be right back."

She didn't, of course, go right back.

She knew that Strome would need some time to himself. Time to adjust to the truth, time to let his heart accept that the woman he'd loved so long ago hadn't betrayed him as he'd believed. Time to let go of the bitterness, time to suffer the new pain, the pain of remorse, for having so misjudged Hazel, who had sacrificed her own happiness—and that of the man she loved and wanted—to stand by the man who needed her.

Nairne stood at the living room window, looking out unseeingly, her brow pressed against the cold pane. He was, after all, her knight in shining armor...no "if only's, no tarnish to contend with. But her elation would have to wait till later; now all she could think of was the agony Strome must be feeling. She glanced at her watch and murmured anxiously. It was more than half an hour since she'd left him in the kitchen; how much longer——?

"Nairne..."

She froze as she heard his voice. Froze, and, with all the will in the world, couldn't turn around. Couldn't face him, couldn't bear to see the ravages of grief, the torment in his eyes...

She didn't hear his step on the carpeted floor, and felt her breath catch in her throat as his arms came around her. "Nairne, look at me."

What was she going to see? I'm afraid to look at you, she wanted to cry. Drawing on all her courage, she turned in his embrace.

His eyes were clear and steady. "Hugh never walked again?"

"No," she whispered. "He spent the rest of his life in a wheelchair."

"And the accident—on the boat——"

"It happened the night before he was to come back to Glencraig. Someone had left a hatch open, and in the dark he fell into the hold. Both his legs were crushed. It was a miracle that he lived."

In the long silence that followed the only sound was the hiss and crackle of the fire. There was a slight tremor in Strome's voice when he finally went on, "So of course he couldn't have come 'striding' back to Hazel. She worded her letter that way on purpose, so that I would never guess..."

"That's right."

Now she noticed the smears on his cheeks, the only sign of the tears he had shed. Her throat almost closed with the pain of it. Closing her eyes, she leaned against him. Warm hands clasped her close.

"It's all over, Nairne. It's all in the past. And I want you to know that it was already in the past for me before I came back today. You see, after I returned to London I felt as if I had left part of myself behind—here in Glencraig, with you, and with Kilty. I'd never in my life had that feeling before—not even with Hazel. And there was so much love in my heart that there was no longer any room for bitterness. I was able to see that what Hazel and I had had together was a little bit of summer madness—and now I can look back on it as just a sweet dream... the nightmare is over. Oh, Nairne, I've made you cry... again."

"I... can't help it..."

He caressed her hair tenderly. "Then let the tears be tears of happiness."

Nairne sobbed quietly, till at last she felt her heart begin to ease. Then, brushing her wet eyelashes with her fingertips, she looked up at Strome with a wavering smile. "They *were* tears of happiness, but they were tears of sadness too. Sadness for Hazel. Every time she looked at Kilty she would have seen you. How it must have hurt... and yet she adored him—they both did. He was a joy to them."

"He asked me, this morning, if I minded him calling me Strome. He said he'll always think of Hugh as his 'dad.' He also said that he doesn't want to keep it a secret that I'm his father—there's no one now who can be hurt by the telling and——" he brushed a hand across his eyes "—he's just so damned proud of me!"

So much emotion in one day; Nairne felt her eyes fil with tears again, but this time she smiled through them.

"Not half as proud as you are going to be of him!" she whispered.

He framed her face between his hands, and with a low moan claimed her lips in a kiss that had her straining against him. A jagged pulse of excitement zigzagged through her, and she reached up, tangling her fingers in his thick, silky hair. At his touch, all her inhibitions had dissipated, and, as she felt his body tremble, passion stormed through her, overwhelming her in wave after wave, so that she wanted nothing more than for his kiss to go on forever. It was a kiss such as she'd never known before; it rocked her, sent her senses reeling. The earth, she was thinking somewhere in a very, very distant part of her mind, didn't move; funny, she would have expected it to...

But, even as the wisp of thought evaporated, all at once her eyes were blinded by a brilliant flashing light that illuminated their private world as if lightning had struck.

Blinking, she drew her lips from Strome's, and in his eyes she could see an awe, an amazement that surely mirrored her own.

"My goodness, Nairne," he breathed, "you're high voltage!"

"You're not exactly low voltage yourself——"

A discreet cough from the direction of the doorway shattered the moment, and they swiveled abruptly, arms still around each other.

Kilty was standing there, his dark hair falling over his brow, the ragged Black Watch tartan kilt slanting over his lean hips. A mischievous grin creased his face and lit up his gray eyes as he leaned lazily against the doorjamb.

Hitching up the kilt with one hand, he dangled his Nikon in front of him with the other.

"Gotcha!" he chuckled.

EPILOGUE

"NAIRNE, your groom has arrived! Did you see him?"

Nairne turned from her bedroom window as her sister came through the doorway, holding out a bouquet of dewy red roses. Kyla's eyes sparkled with excitement.

"I was worried," she said breathlessly, "in case Strome might forget to bring your bouquet when he flew up from London, but I should have known better, since he was the one who insisted that Glencraig wouldn't be able to come up with a floral arrangement good enough for... what was it he called you? Ah, yes, his 'own sweet flower'!"

Nairne laughed. "So you've noticed that my city man can wax poetic at times." She took the bouquet and held it to her nostrils, closing her eyes as she inhaled the exquisite fragrance. "Oh, they're perfect!"

Turning again to look out of the window, she said, "Yes, I did see Strome arrive—the very first to use his new landing pad. Is Adam ready to drive him to the kirk?"

"Mm. They're waiting for me in the living room. Dad insisted on pouring a wee dram for Strome to shore him up!"

Grinning, Nairne slid an arm around her sister's waist, and together they looked over the fields at the new Crest Mountain Lodge... and at the beautiful granite house Strome had built for his bride on the old site of the Craigend farmhouse, a house whose front windows looked down the glen and across the loch. From his bedroom Kilty would be able to look up and see the majestic peak of his beloved Slagmhor. Nairne was going to run Bruach as a teenage center, and Strome was going to base his business in Glencraig. He would never again say that home was where he hung his hat, Nairne reflected contentedly; his home would be where he wanted it to be...here, in Glencraig, with her.

"Strome said the complex would take a year to build," Kyla murmured. "And he was right—almost to the day."

"It's been a wonderful year," Nairne said softly. "Kilty's so happy—and Strome——"

"You melted his heart," Kyla said, "with your sweetness and your goodness..."

She paused, and frowned as she heard Nairne give a wistful little sigh. "What is it?" she asked, a hint of anxiety in her voice. "Surely there's nothing...wrong?"

"Oh, no——" Nairne broke off with a grimace, and hesitated for a moment before saying, "I know it'll sound silly..." She made a frustrated little sound. "It's just that I've been thinking about the past while I've been up here alone. Thinking about...Rory." She bit her lip, felt her cheeks flush. "You see, he still has a corner of my heart...and always will. I'm...going to have to tell Strome. But I'm afraid...afraid he won't understand."

Kyla hugged her sister tightly. "Oh, you silly goose! How could you underestimate Strome so? I'm sure he realizes that your kind of woman doesn't just cast aside her memories in such a casual way. Now, no more sad thoughts on this special day. Smile, and——" she adjusted the lace collar of Nairne's cream silk dress "—now I really must go. Give us five minutes or so, then you and Dad follow on." After giving her sister a last quick hug she crossed the room and, going out, closed the door behind her.

The smile slowly faded from Nairne's face. "Oh, Strome," she murmured, holding the roses to her nostrils again, "how can I love you with all my heart and still——?"

She froze as she looked down at the glorious bouquet. She had thought it contained only roses, red roses...

But there, nestled among them, so nearly hidden that it was almost a miracle that she had noticed them, were several snowdrops. Small and dainty, they were the most beautiful she had ever seen.

Her breath caught in her throat, and for a moment she thought she might choke. *Strome must have put them there.* Was this why he had insisted on being the one to order her bouquet? Had he wanted her to know, on their wedding day, that he knew how she felt, understood how she felt, and that he would never expect her to close her heart to her memories of Rory?

She thought she had loved Strome before; now she felt her heart spilling over. So much love she had in it, enough for Strome... and enough for Kilty too, for Kyla and Adam, the children, her parents...

And for Rory.

But Strome had known all along what she had just learned—what he had taught her with his gift of the snowdrops. A heart could hold more than just a heartful of love; it could be full to overflowing...

There was quite a crowd gathered outside the church, and as Nairne and her father approached the open doorway she saw Fanny Webster among the spectators, staring at her avidly from behind her thick-lensed glasses. Their eyes met, and at exactly that moment Nairne felt the faintest little fluttering in the region of her stomach. The first little fluttering. An unfamiliar little fluttering. But, unfamiliar though it was, she knew only too well what had caused it... and it wasn't butterflies...

Excitement flared through her... and her lips curved in a mischievous smile. In a month or two Fanny Webster was indeed going to have something to gossip about!

Nairne's mouth still held the hint of a smile as she walked slowly, gracefully down the center aisle on her father's arm, her bouquet held tenderly before her, but her eyes—eyes that went straight to Strome—were just a little misted.

He was standing before the minister, with Kilty—his best man—close at his side. Both looked incredibly handsome in full Highland dress, and both turned to gaze on her as she drew near. Kilty's face was bright with joy, and Strome's... the love in his blue eyes set her heartbeats bumping about as if they wanted to get there before her. Was it possible, she wondered dizzily, to die of sheer ecstasy?

"Easy now, lass..." Her father murmured the steadying words as she almost stumbled. "Easy..."

Yes, Nairne thought as she stood up beside Strome, heard his lightly breathed "Lord, you're so beautiful!", yes, it was going to be easy. Easy to love this man, easy to be loved by him.

The rich, sweet fragrance of the red roses scented the air as the minister began reading the sacred words that would make her Strome's wife, and bless their union forever.

IT'S FREE! IT'S FUN! ENTER THE

☆ "Hooray for ☆
☆ Hollywood" ☆

SWEEPSTAKES!

We're giving away prizes to celebrate the screening of four new romance movies on CBS TV this fall! Look for the movies on four Sunday afternoons in October. And be sure to return your Official Entry Coupons to try for a fabulous **vacation in Hollywood!**

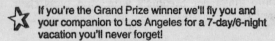 If you're the Grand Prize winner we'll fly you and your companion to Los Angeles for a 7-day/6-night vacation you'll never forget!

You'll stay at the luxurious Regent Beverly Wilshire Hotel,* a prime location for celebrity spotting!

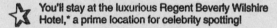 You'll have time to visit Universal Studios,* stroll the Hollywood Walk of Fame, check out celebrities' footprints at Mann's Chinese Theater, ride a trolley to see the homes of the stars, and more!

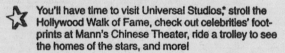 The prize includes a rental car for 7 days and $1,000.00 pocket money!

Someone's going to win this fabulous prize, and it might just be you! Remember, the more times you enter, the better your chances of winning!

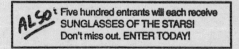 Five hundred entrants will each receive SUNGLASSES OF THE STARS! Don't miss out. ENTER TODAY!

The proprietors of the trademark are not associated with this promotion.

Take 4 bestselling love stories FREE

Plus get a FREE surprise gift!

Special Limited-time Offer

Mail to Harlequin Reader Service®

3010 Walden Avenue
P.O. Box 1867
Buffalo, N.Y. 14269-1867

YES! Please send me 4 free Harlequin Presents® novels and my free surprise gift. Then send me 6 brand-new novels every month, which I will receive months before they appear in bookstores. Bill me at the low price of $2.44 each plus 25¢ delivery and applicable sales tax, if any*. That's the complete price and—compared to the cover prices of $2.99 each—quite a bargain! I understand that accepting the books and gift places me under no obligation ever to buy any books. I can always return a shipment and cancel at any time. Even if I never buy another book from Harlequin, the 4 free books and the surprise gift are mine to keep forever.

106 BPA ANRH

Name	(PLEASE PRINT)	
Address	Apt. No.	
City	State	Zip

This offer is limited to one order per household and not valid to present Harlequin Presents® subscribers. *Terms and prices are subject to change without notice. Sales tax applicable in N.Y.

UPRES-94R   ©1990 Harlequin Enterprises Limited

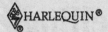 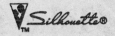

The movie event of the season can be the reading event of the year!

Lights... The lights go on in October when CBS presents Harlequin/Silhouette Sunday Matinee Movies. These four movies are based on bestselling Harlequin and Silhouette novels.

Camera... As the cameras roll, be the first to read the original novels the movies are based on!

Action... Through this offer, you can have these books sent directly to you! Just fill in the order form below and you could be reading the books...before the movie!

48288-4	Treacherous Beauties by Cheryl Emerson	
	$3.99 U.S./$4.50 CAN.	☐
83305-9	Fantasy Man by Sharon Green	
	$3.99 U.S./$4.50 CAN.	☐
48289-2	A Change of Place by Tracy Sinclair	
	$3.99 U.S./$4.50CAN.	☐
83306-7	Another Woman by Margot Dalton	
	$3.99 U.S./$4.50 CAN.	☐

TOTAL AMOUNT	$
POSTAGE & HANDLING	$
($1.00 for one book, 50¢ for each additional)	
APPLICABLE TAXES*	$_____
TOTAL PAYABLE	$_____
(check or money order—please do not send cash)	

To order, complete this form and send it, along with a check or money order for the total above, payable to Harlequin Books, to: **In the U.S.:** 3010 Walden Avenue, P.O. Box 9047, Buffalo, NY 14269-9047; **In Canada:** P.O. Box 613, Fort Erie, Ontario, L2A 5X3.

Name: _____

Address: _____ City: _____

State/Prov.: _____ Zip/Postal Code: _____

*New York residents remit applicable sales taxes.
  Canadian residents remit applicable GST and provincial taxes.

CBSPR

"HOORAY FOR HOLLYWOOD" SWEEPSTAKES

HERE'S HOW THE SWEEPSTAKES WORKS

OFFICIAL RULES — NO PURCHASE NECESSARY

To enter, complete an Official Entry Form or hand print on a 3" x 5" card the words "HOORAY FOR HOLLYWOOD", your name and address and mail your entry in the pre-addressed envelope (if provided) or to: "Hooray for Hollywood" Sweepstakes, P.O. Box 9076, Buffalo, NY 14269-9076 or "Hooray for Hollywood" Sweepstakes, P.O. Box 637, Fort Erie, Ontario L2A 5X3. Entries must be sent via First Class Mail and be received no later than 12/31/94. No liability is assumed for lost, late or misdirected mail.

Winners will be selected in random drawings to be conducted no later than January 31, 1995 from all eligible entries received.

Grand Prize: A 7-day/6-night trip for 2 to Los Angeles, CA including round trip air transportation from commercial airport nearest winner's residence, accommodations at the Regent Beverly Wilshire Hotel, free rental car, and $1,000 spending money. (Approximate prize value which will vary dependent upon winner's residence: $5,400.00 U.S.); 500 Second Prizes: A pair of "Hollywood Star" sunglasses (prize value: $9.95 U.S. each). Winner selection is under the supervision of D.L. Blair, Inc., an independent judging organization, whose decisions are final. Grand Prize travelers must sign and return a release of liability prior to traveling. Trip must be taken by 2/1/96 and is subject to airline schedules and accommodations availability.

Sweepstakes offer is open to residents of the U.S. (except Puerto Rico) and Canada who are 18 years of age or older, except employees and immediate family members of Harlequin Enterprises, Ltd., its affiliates, subsidiaries, and all agencies, entities or persons connected with the use, marketing or conduct of this sweepstakes. All federal, state, provincial, municipal and local laws apply. Offer void wherever prohibited by law. Taxes and/or duties are the sole responsibility of the winners. Any litigation within the province of Quebec respecting the conduct and awarding of prizes may be submitted to the Regie des loteries et courses du Quebec. All prizes will be awarded; winners will be notified by mail. No substitution of prizes are permitted. Odds of winning are dependent upon the number of eligible entries received.

Potential grand prize winner must sign and return an Affidavit of Eligibility within 30 days of notification. In the event of non-compliance within this time period, prize may be awarded to an alternate winner. Prize notification returned as undeliverable may result in the awarding of prize to an alternate winner. By acceptance of their prize, winners consent to use of their names, photographs, or likenesses for purpose of advertising, trade and promotion on behalf of Harlequin Enterprises, Ltd., without further compensation unless prohibited by law. A Canadian winner must correctly answer an arithmetical skill-testing question in order to be awarded the prize.

For a list of winners (available after 2/28/95), send a separate stamped, self-addressed envelope to: Hooray for Hollywood Sweepstakes 3252 Winners, P.O. Box 4200, Blair, NE 68009.

CBSRLS

OFFICIAL ENTRY COUPON

"Hooray for Hollywood"
SWEEPSTAKES!

Yes, I'd love to win the Grand Prize — a vacation in Hollywood —
or one of 500 pairs of "sunglasses of the stars"! Please enter me
in the sweepstakes!

This entry must be received by December 31, 1994.
Winners will be notified by January 31, 1995.

Name _____

Address _____ Apt. _____

City _____

State/Prov. _____ Zip/Postal Code _____

Daytime phone number _____
(area code)

Mail all entries to: Hooray for Hollywood Sweepstakes,
P.O. Box 9076, Buffalo, NY 14269-9076.
In Canada, mail to: Hooray for Hollywood Sweepstakes,
P.O. Box 637, Fort Erie, ON L2A 5X3.

KCH

OFFICIAL ENTRY COUPON

"Hooray for Hollywood"
SWEEPSTAKES!

Yes, I'd love to win the Grand Prize — a vacation in Hollywood —
or one of 500 pairs of "sunglasses of the stars"! Please enter me
in the sweepstakes!

This entry must be received by December 31, 1994.
Winners will be notified by January 31, 1995.

Name _____

Address _____ Apt. _____

City _____

State/Prov. _____ Zip/Postal Code _____

Daytime phone number _____
(area code)

Mail all entries to: Hooray for Hollywood Sweepstakes,
P.O. Box 9076, Buffalo, NY 14269-9076.
In Canada, mail to: Hooray for Hollywood Sweepstakes,
P.O. Box 637, Fort Erie, ON L2A 5X3.

KCH